Never
Finished

A small town opposites attract romance

Ana Rhodes

Stardust Publishing LLC

Contents

Emma

"That sounds fabulous," I enthused with a smile that made my cheeks feel like they would break. I detested that feeling. I used to smile warmly and genuinely, but I didn't have it in me to put in the effort.

Truthfully, I hadn't felt the energy to put much effort into anything lately. I suppose I could blame it on feeling adrift ever since my mom passed away—or I could blame it on hunger. These business dinners almost always involved some minuscule serving of what amounted to a gourmet cracker with a teaspoon of pureed meat and a sprig of whatever was in season draped across it.

My client continued to go on about some new spa treatment that didn't interest me in the slightest and I bit back at a smile as I remembered an old friend who used to call it "rich people food." He'd teased the meager servings were why rich people were so thin. He'd said they consumed nothing but "petrified shingles with some sauce, along with a martini."

Jaime had always had a colorful way of describing the world around him. I missed that—and Jaime—a lot. Perhaps too much for someone I hadn't seen in twelve years. The last time I saw Jaime Acosta, he'd left me dizzy with the deepest, most soul-searing kiss I'd ever had, and no one has come close since. So, I guess it wasn't too surprising he popped into my head as frequently as he did.

Like then, I remembered how I frequented the local diner just because Jaime was a cook there—and how badly I could go for one of those burger, fries, and shake combos right now.

Mercifully, I steered my client back to business and wrapped things up. Soon, I was standing alone outside the restaurant. It was early fall in Colorado, and having spent most of the last decade in Los Angeles, I'd forgotten how cool it got that time of year.

It was a little nerve-racking being back in Colorado, and I blamed my thoughts of Jaime on being so close to home. Thankfully, I wasn't back in Silverpine. Being in my hometown would be far too difficult, especially since my mother died.

One thing I could take comfort in was the knowledge I wouldn't have to drive far before I stumbled on a greasy diner. With all the truckers who ran through our state, diners were a staple, and while I doubted any place could compete with Mabel's Diner in Silverpine, I was certain

I could find something ten times better than what I'd just consumed.

I went in the opposite direction of my hotel and kept my eyes peeled for any telltale signs of what my stomach was growling for.

Sure enough, not far out of town, I saw the familiar sign of a half-moon, which directed me to Gus's Bar and Grill.

The parking lot was mostly gravel, and as I slid my rental BMW into a spot in front of the building, I was a little embarrassed by the stark difference between it and the beat-up cars and trucks dotting the haphazard parking lot.

I'd been born with money, but I'd never felt like I had a silver spoon in my mouth. My parents grew their wealth from the ground up. My father cashed in a small portion of the land my mother's family owned and built Pine Crest Mountain Resort. It was now one of the premier ski resorts in Colorado—and I was carrying on my mom's legacy as the head of business development.

My mom's family had been in the state of Colorado since before it had been settled. They had thousands of acres of land and worked it diligently, even through the Great Depression and the countless blizzards that had threatened their homestead.

My mom could identify every tree, deer track, and bird call—she'd loved nature, which rubbed off on me. She'd loved it so much her first job was as a nature guide, and as fate would have it, my father was in one of her tour groups.

He was almost ten years older than her, and I sometimes wondered what attracted them to one another. But then, I knew my father—he had charm for days and an easy smile, and he could be loving and giving to a fault. But there was also a hard edge to him. He could be brutal when it came to business, and my mother had always had a way of softening his edges.

Unfortunately, since she'd passed away, there was no softening of those edges, and John Carter was not mellowing with age. It was all business all the time now, and he didn't care who he had to squash to make a deal.

I was becoming increasingly alarmed by his thirst. I tried to employ some of the same tactics my mother used, but she'd had the magic touch. Every time I tried to calm him, he'd snap and say, "This is the way business is done. You need to toughen up and take that heart off your sleeve, or you're never going to make it, much less take over the company."

I had to give my father credit. He took that piece of land my mother gave him and built the grandest resort the state of Colorado had ever seen. Our resort hosted more celebrities, debutants, and suspected mob bosses than I could count. If you were famous or had money to burn, you were welcome at Pine Crest Mountain.

Regrettably, that rubbed my mom the wrong way. She wanted Pine Crest to be a place where families could have fun and enjoy the beautiful bounty that was Colorado. But that didn't change that my father had made a success out of the place.

Toward the end of her life, my dad had begun nagging her to sign over the rest of her land. I knew he had thoughts about expanding into a mega-resort. But as much as she'd had a soft spot for my father, my mother signed the land over to me, and it has become a source of contention between my father and me.

He's been in my ear about how much money we could make off that land, but for the first time in my life, I found the strength to put my foot down, and I told him I would honor Mom's wishes. I didn't want to see all that beautiful land bulldozed.

Even though I knew I did the right thing, I felt guilty. I only had one parent left, and he was upset with me. So I've been working my butt off to prove to my father I could be a savvy businesswoman, especially as he talked more and more about eventually handing me the reins. The problem was, I wasn't sure I wanted to take over. It was easy to think about the things I could do with the company if I was in charge. I could make our resorts more accessible to regular families and more kid-friendly, just as my mom wanted. But it was also a huge responsibility.

I wasn't about to admit any of that to my dad because he'd have a fit. I would, however, prove to him I was more than capable of managing our business.

It came at a cost, though. I was lonely, exhausted, and still grieving. So much so, my best friends, Caroline and Sophie, tried to talk me out of coming on the trip. They'd suggested I tell my dad somebody else should take the lead, but I wasn't about to let that happen. I knew if I turned it down, he'd believe I didn't have the courage to be CEO one day. So I did what I do best, put on a happy face and got the deal done. Being back in my home state wasn't all terrible. It was nice to see a Colorado sunset again, even if it made my heart ache for things that might've been.

As soon as I entered the diner, the smell of grease, meat, and sugar hit my nose. I inhaled deeply, drinking it into my veins. My mouth practically watered in anticipation of what I was about to order.

A tired looking waitress handed me a sticky menu and directed me to a booth where I happily slid across the cracked vinyl seat and poured over the menu, tempted to order it all. But I settled for my old standby: a burger, fries, and chocolate milkshake. It was my celebration dinner for surviving my trip to Colorado.

Tomorrow, I would be on the first flight back to LA, and I could pretend there wasn't a gigantic piece of land beckoning me home. I could throw myself into work and pretend my mom wasn't gone, and maybe if I was really lucky, I could fool myself into pretending Jaime and I had never been friends.

I smiled to myself ruefully. I didn't really want to do that. As much as it pained me to remember what I'd given up, I wouldn't give up my memories with Jaime for anything. It was odd how those memories could both torture and comfort me in my darkest times.

I struggled to accept I was a thirty-year-old woman pining for someone in I knew in high school. Sure, we'd stolen a few moments, and sometimes I believed we could have been more, but in the end, we were friends.

I often complained I could never seem to move on from him. There was always the ghost of Jaime, and nobody could ever live up to it. My girlfriends coined it the "Jaime Effect." I would date a guy for a while, and everything would go great until I found a frivolous reason to break up with them. Caroline was the one who came up with the name, and when I questioned her about it, Sophie backed her up and said, "She's right. Nobody can live up to Jaime Acosta. I would love to meet this guy someday and find out if he actually lives up to the hype."

They weren't wrong. Every time I got close to someone, I couldn't help but think of Jaime and what our lives would be like if I'd stood up to my father.

The waitress plopped an oversized plate with a half-pound burger and a generous helping of fries in front of me, then slid a fountain glass with my chocolate shake and a stripy straw across the table.

I resisted the urge to clap like a delighted child and thanked her before digging in. After my first bite, I was quietly moaning to myself when my phone buzzed.

It was a Zoom reminder, and I remembered it was Wednesday night. Caroline, Sophie, and I had a standing appointment so that no matter how busy we were, we had a dedicated time to get caught up. If one of us was traveling, we'd video conference, but if we were all in the city, we'd sip margaritas and munch on chips and salsa at one of our apartments, usually Sophie's because she had the best view.

I grabbed my earbuds out of my purse and slipped them into my ears so I wouldn't disturb the other diners as I logged into the Zoom conference. Their familiar loving faces appeared on my small screen, and I beamed at them. Whatever I thought I'd missed out on being an only child growing up, Sophie and Caroline filled the void. They were more than my best friends. They were my soul sisters, and I don't think I'd still be upright after my mom died if it wasn't for them.

"Did you think we were going to let you get away with not taking part in the usual meet?" Sophie asked with a raised eyebrow.

I grinned at them. "Oh, I know that would never happen—I just forgot what day it was," I admitted.

Caroline gasped dramatically and put a hand to her chest. "How dare you," she said, fighting back a smile.

I shook my head. "I know, I know. It's just my head is all screwed up being back here."

Sophie and Caroline both nodded in understanding from their respective screens when I realized they weren't together. "Wait. Where are you two?"

"Well, I'm in John's apartment," Sophie said.

Caroline and I glanced at one another, pasting on fake smiles. Sophie had just started dating the guy, and he was all she talked about. He seemed nice enough, but both Caroline and I got a weird vibe from him we couldn't quite put a finger on yet. We were nervous for our friend because she was over the moon in love.

All we could do was caution her to go slow, but she wasn't hearing any of that. As far as she was concerned, Caroline was just a workaholic who wasn't interested in any kind of relationship, and I was still madly in love with a boy I used to know.

"And as you can see," Caroline said, cutting into my thoughts and changing the subject, "I am in the dungeon otherwise known as work."

"Do you ever leave there before nine?" I asked her in disbelief.

She rolled her eyes and shook her head. "You're one to talk. You're having to dance a jig for work every time I blink," Caroline groused.

"There's a difference," I said, swirling a fry through my puddle of ketchup. "I have the joy of working for my father, which means there are complex family dynamics and dysfunction at play here. You just work for a corporation that mercilessly sucks you dry every chance it gets. "

Caroline laughed. "I think that's just the way work is for everyone," she pointed out.

"Not me," Sophie said.

Caroline and I both shared an eye roll as Caroline spit out, "Yes, well, when you're your own boss, it's a little different, isn't it? I'm sure even you find your boss irritating sometimes—I sure do," she smirked.

Sophie rolled her eyes. "You can abuse me all you want. I'm just saying if something bothers you that much, it's up to you to change it."

"She's not wrong, Lina," I admitted to Caroline.

Caroline shook her head. "Whatever, save the spiel for another day. We need to check in on Miss Emma here. She's the one several states away doing her father's bidding ... again. How's it going out there?"

I felt tears prick the back of my eyes. It wasn't like I hadn't felt the urge to cry since I'd stepped off the airplane and onto Colorado soil for the first time in over two years, but having my best friends looking at me with concern made everything rise to the surface.

"Oh, hey, we're not trying to make you upset," Caroline insisted.

I shook my head, trying to stave off the tears. "No, it's not that. I just really miss her. And I can feel her everywhere. I'm so embarrassed. I can barely handle being here without her, and I'm not even in Silverpine."

My friends nodded sympathetically. Caroline had gone through the pain of losing her father, so she knew better than most. And Sophie was one of the most empathetic people I knew. Plus, they both got to know Lydia Carter themselves, and they loved her, too. It was impossible not to be crazy about my mom.

"Well, on the bright side, you'll be back in LA by this time tomorrow. And we'll take you out for a proper dinner," Sophie said, having caught sight of the plate in front of me.

"I'll have you know this is fine Colorado fare. Nowhere near as good as Mabel's, but I'm enjoying it."

Both were laughing now. "Oh, no, it could never be as good as Mabel's," Caroline deadpanned. "Or is it never as good as the *hot* cook making you a burger on the spot? Are you going to look up Jaime while you're there?" Sophie asked, only half teasing.

I laughed. "Please, he probably doesn't even remember me."

"Excuse me?" Caroline challenged, raising an eyebrow, "I saw pictures of you in high school, and if that boy doesn't remember the smoking hot redhead with curves for days, he's an idiot not to be messed with anyway."

I smiled. "You two are too much sometimes."

"But the best kind," Sophie sang.

I was still laughing when we were interrupted by an incoming call from "Dad."

"Uh oh, what's that face?" Caroline asked, worried.

I sucked in a breath. "Nothing, it's just my Dad. You know how he is if I make him wait."

My friends rolled their eyes and shook their heads.

"Yep, you better answer that, or the old Sarge will have a fit," Caroline said, using the nickname many people used for my dad. He'd long been called Sarge even though he'd never served in the military—he just had a drill sergeant's attitude.

"I hate to cut this short …"

Sophie put up her hands. "Say no more, but feel free to call us back when you're done with your dad if you need to talk."

I nodded. "Just a few more hours," I said, pasting a bright smile on my face and saying my goodbyes before answering my dad.

"Hey, Dad, what's up?" I answered with fake cheer as I eyed my now cold burger in front of me.

"I heard you did a fine job with the Airoldi account this evening, and I wanted to call to congratulate my girl," he said, and even though he was patting me on the back, metaphorically speaking, I could sense there was more.

"Yeah, it was a cinch, just as I said it would be."

"Atta girl," he encouraged. "In fact, they were so impressed with you, it makes me more comfortable giving you this next assignment."

I laughed, "I just finished your last assignment an hour ago, Dad."

"No rest for the wicked," he said, which always put me on edge.

"Right, of course," I conceded.

"This one's going to keep you in Colorado for a little longer, which is why I wanted to get a hold of you tonight before you got on that plane in the morning."

"What? What on earth could keep me in Colorado?"

"I thought you'd like this assignment because it'll take you back to the flagship resort."

My heart sank even as it began thudding harder in my chest. The flagship resort—that was how my father always referred to it—not my childhood home or Pine Crest. Once again, it was all business for him.

I waited with bated breath as he explained. "I've been working on a merger for some time that has some complex details to it. It's been a real bear to deal with. But I think I'm closing in on an agreement that will make everybody happy—and very rich."

I huffed out a laugh. "Please, Dad, we're already very rich," I mumbled, not wanting anyone to overhear that bit.

"Can you ever be too rich?" he chuckled.

Apparently not.

"Mr. Travers is sending his son, Andrew Jr., to the flagship resort for a few days, and I'm hoping you'll be able to schmooze him a bit and work over the finer points of the details. I'll send you what I have so far. I want you to be your best for this, Emma."

"Aren't I always?" I asked.

"I'm serious, Emma. This has the potential to change everything for the company. Plus, I've met this young man. He's a good sort of fellow, and I think you two would hit it off."

I didn't like how sounded. Was he trying to set me up?

"That's all well and good, Dad, but let's just keep it to business. Okay?"

"I'm just saying, dear girl, it doesn't hurt to keep an open mind. He's young, rich, and successful, and I'm man enough to admit he's pretty easy on the eyes, too."

"Dad!"

"Okay, okay. I'll quit pushing. But don't rule out the possibility just because I said something about it. I'm forwarding the details to your inbox as we speak. My secretary has already prepared the family suite, and I'll have her cancel your flight for tomorrow. Now you have a dinner date—sorry, a meeting with Mr. Travers Jr. tomorrow at seven, but I want you there with plenty of time to prepare and reacquaint yourself with the property."

I bit back a laugh. "Right," I said. I wouldn't need to reacquaint myself with Pine Crest Mountain. I knew that place and the surrounding land like the back of my hand. It had been my playground, my home as a child, and more recently, the place I'd been avoiding. "How long do you think it's going to take, Dad?" I asked anxiously.

"Oh, I wouldn't worry about your other work, Emma. This deal is of the utmost importance. Anything you have scheduled in LA can be delegated to somebody else or postponed."

Great. The few days I'd already spent in Colorado were hard enough, and now I was headed home to the one place I'd been avoiding. And I would have to do it with a damn smile on my face.

My dad gave me a few more details and then signed off. Suddenly, that burger, fries, and shake sat in my stomach like a lead weight.

Since I'd left Silverpine for college, I'd only returned to Pine Crest to visit my mom, and those visits were brief. Despite trying to avoid all the places that reminded me of Jaime, he was everywhere. So, while my father was off gallivanting in the name of business, I would stick close to the resort and my mother's side.

Although we'd never spoke of it, she knew how painful it was for me to return and understood what I'd given up. She was my security blanket, and I didn't know how I would survive the visit without her. Now I'd have to face two ghosts—alone.

I paid the waitress, gave her a generous tip, even though I left half my food uneaten, and shuffled back to my car.

As I pulled out of the gravel parking lot, tears started streaming down my face. I blinked them away, trying to concentrate on the unfamiliar road leading back to my hotel.

"Only a few more minutes," I coached myself as the impending panic and anxiety threatened to overtake me. I was well practiced at pushing those feelings aside, but lately, it was getting harder to keep them at bay.

I kept my head down as I walked through the hotel lobby and rode up the elevator to my room on the seventh floor. Only when I shut the hotel room door and locked it behind me did I allow the tears to flow freely.

I'd only been in my room for a couple of minutes when my phone started ringing. It was a group call from Sophie and Caroline. Somehow, they always knew when I needed them. Of course, knowing I was just talking to my father, it was a safe bet I would need some moral support.

I contemplated not answering. They were going to know I was crying, and there was no avoiding it. I wasn't certain I wanted to share what was going on, but they would find out eventually, so I sucked in a deep breath and answered.

"Hey, I hope we're not bothering you again too soon," Caroline started, "but Sophie sent out the bat signal. She said she could sense a change in your aura or whatever and insisted you needed us."

I heard Sophie huff over the line as I answered in a shaky voice, "She was right." Then I burst into tears.

"How do you do that?" Caroline asked Sophie.

"It's a gift and a burden," Sophie replied. "Emma, it's going to be okay. Take some deep breaths, and when you're ready, tell us what happened."

I couldn't stop crying, and it came out all garbled, but somehow, they understood when I said, "Okay, but it's going to be a minute. Or five."

"Okay. But after that, we'll be here to redirect you because, while it's totally fine to cry when you're sad, you never want to do it for too long, or you'll make yourself sick."

"My mother always said that," I blubbered, and Caroline groaned.

"There I go again, saying the wrong thing."

"No, no, it's okay. I just …" I sucked in a deep breath, then relayed the phone conversation I had with my father. Anyone else probably wouldn't have been able to decipher what I was saying, but I was pretty sure I shared information telepathically with those two, so they would understand.

"Wow," Sophie breathed once I was done. "That's an awful lot to ask of you, Emma."

"No shit," Caroline agreed, and I could hear the anger bubbling up in her voice, but she was trying to keep it in check for me. It wouldn't be the first time Caroline went on an angry rant about my father, but she wasn't saying anything I didn't already know.

"What are you going to do, Emma?" Sophie asked, and I could hear the worry in her voice.

"I don't think I have much of a choice… I'm going home."

Jaime

"**A**lright everybody, last call," I hollered, looking at the sparse crowd left in the bar. It was a Wednesday, so there weren't that many people left, and most of the regular business diners had already gone up to their rooms.

The Lounge at Pine Crest Mountain Resort was the most luxurious bar I'd ever worked in. It also paid the best, which was the only reason I was there. My family needed the money, so I worked where I was reminded every day of the girl who got away.

Guests began settling their tabs and filing out of the bar. My assistant manager, Charlie, finished cleaning up and preparing for the next day while I balanced the books.

It was probably my least favorite part of the job. When I'd gotten my mixology certification, the last thing I thought I'd be doing was balancing ledgers, but it was part of being management—and management brought in the money. And every dollar I had to spare went to help my mom.

I'd sent money home for years. Before my dad passed away, he'd reminded me I would be the man of the house, and it would be my responsibility to make sure my mom and sisters were taken care of. I took my promise to him seriously … but I didn't need to stay in Silverpine to provide for my family. So, I bounced around California hustling, getting my certification and gaining a reputation while still sending a weekly allowance home.

My sisters gave me a lot of shit for leaving Silverpine, but my heart couldn't take it. With memories of my father and Emma lurking around every corner, I was better off anywhere but there.

A flash of red startled me out of my thoughts, and I jerked my head up to catch a petite redhead walking past the lounge entrance. The bar was dimly lit this time of night, so I couldn't decide if it was the right shade of red, but the possibility it was her made my heart race.

I felt a nudge on my shoulder and looked up at Charlie, who shook his head before mumbling, "It's not her, boss."

At that moment, the redhead turned around—it wasn't Emma. I returned to the task at hand, clearing my throat as I mumbled, "I wasn't thinking that."

"If you say so," Charlie said, giving the bar a final wipe down. "But I've seen that look before."

"What look?" I asked, irritated although I knew exactly what he was referring to. He was one of the few people who could spot when I was spiraling, which happened almost every time I was reminded of Emma. Unfortunately, it'd become a regular thing since I returned to Silverpine.

Charlie was one of the few faces I was relieved to see when I came home to help take care of my mother. He was the first friend I'd made when my family immigrated from Spain.

It might've seemed odd to settle in a quiet ski town in Colorado when we could have gone anywhere, but my parents thought Silverpine felt a lot like Navacerrada, the town we'd left. It was a safe place to raise a family, and there was plenty of opportunity for a hardworking, resourceful immigrant like him. My father was convinced we'd have a better life in America.

I'd wondered about that a lot over the years because, in many ways, it didn't feel better. But the one time I dared to speak my doubts out loud, my mother was livid and scolded me, "You have no idea what we sacrificed to get you here. You should be grateful."

While she never gave us specifics on what exactly they'd given up, we never questioned her. It was an unwritten rule in our household. That was why I had to laugh when my father told me I was the "man of the house" because everybody in the Acosta family knew Mama was the boss.

But now my mother could barely remember her own name, and while she was more docile now that the dementia had settled in, I missed the fiery woman who never let me get away with anything.

Late one night a few months ago, I'd gotten a call from my little sister Maria, and she'd simply said, "It's time to come home, Jaime."

I could tell by the exhaustion in her voice there would be no arguing. I'd put off coming back for years, always finding an excuse, but the truth was it was easier to stay away. In Silverpine, there was no avoiding what I'd lost—or what I was about to lose.

Charlie had been there for it all.

He'd warned me back then not to get involved with that "Carter girl," not because he didn't like her—I didn't know anyone who didn't love Emma—but because he knew her father would never allow her to hang out with "the help" or, in my case, the help's son.

My father was the primary contractor working on the expansion of Pine Crest Mountain Resort, and occasionally, I'd help on the weekends.

I'd noticed the beautiful redhead in the halls of our high school long before I saw her on the jobsite, but I'd never gotten that close to her. I'd watched her with her mother, leaving for hikes on the land behind the resorts and then coming to check on the progress of the construction project. They were always very sweet and supportive, telling the guys what a good job they were doing. Mrs. Carter would often bring doughnuts and coffee or other treats while Mr. Carter's reception was less than welcoming.

Emma amazed me by how easily she could talk to anybody. Most teenagers were awkward and had a hard time speaking in public, but she spoke to everyone, young and old, male and female, as if they were her new best friend. It was obvious she'd gotten that from her mother. She didn't act like a spoiled rich girl.

Every time I saw her outside of school, she had a beanie or bandanna tied around her head, sporting hiking boots and shorts with a t-shirt. She hardly looked like the princess of Pine Crest. I would later find out just how much she detested that nickname.

I couldn't resist her, though. I'd heeded Charlie's warning back then and played the long game, becoming Emma's friend instead of asking her out. But there was no doubt in my mind, I fell in love with her the first time I saw her on that construction site.

And I was still crazy about her. It was pathetic really. It had been twelve years since she'd left Silverpine. Twelve years of missing her and wondering what our lives would've been like if her father hadn't intervened … or if she'd been able to stand up to him.

"Look, if you ask me, you dodged a bullet," Charlie said as he finished his cleanup ritual. "I mean, she was a nice girl, but you wouldn't have wanted to marry into that family," he said, shaking off a shiver. "Imagine all the crap you'd have to deal with on holidays. Can you really imagine your family sitting around the table with her family? They're polar opposites."

I shook my head even though I'd imagined those very scenarios countless times before. Unbeknownst to Charlie or Emma, I'd imagined a million different dream lives shared with her in the years since she'd left. Maybe I was a masochist, but I couldn't stop myself. However, at that moment, I recognized I needed get a hold of myself because it was getting ridiculous. I was a grown man pining after a dream that never came true.

"Look, I know you don't agree with me," Charlie started. "But you can cut yourself some slack and not give yourself whiplash every time you see a redhead walk through the door. You and I both know the likelihood of Emma Carter coming back to Silverpine is a million-to-one."

Maybe he was right. I'd heard through the grapevine she'd only visited a handful of times, and that was just to see her mother. But since Lydia Carter had passed away a couple of years ago, nobody had seen or heard from Emma.

According to the gossip mill, she'd worked her way up the ranks of the family business and was now considered her father's right hand woman, set to take over as CEO when her father retires. That thought left me with mixed feelings. I was proud of her for accomplishing so much in such a short time, and I knew well enough to know she'd earned it. Mr. Carter didn't hand out anything to anyone, not even his only child. She had a knack for talking to people and getting them to see her point of view.

However, knowing she worked so closely with a man who despised me from the moment we met simply because I was an immigrant and didn't come from a wealthy family irritated me. I had to remind myself that it was where she wanted to be—where she chose to be—and I didn't have to like it.

Someday, I wouldn't have to humble myself by working for the company and the man who ruined my life. Someday, I would have a bar of my own, with my own signature recipes and a warm family vibe. I had to keep my eye on the prize. Right now, every spare dollar I had was paying for Mom's in-home nurse. But once I got more established, I'd be able to save a little more and get out of the hold Pine Crest and Emma Carter had on me.

Emma

♥

I 'd stayed up late the night before on the phone with Sophie and Caroline as they tried to talk me down and felt bolstered as I drove toward Silverpine though that resolve took some hard hits as I saw familiar sites. The last time I'd been in town was to lay my mother to rest. As soon as I shook the hand of the final well-wisher at her funeral, I got my ass out there so fast, I was pretty sure I made a few heads spin.

There was something simultaneously comforting and haunting about breathing in the pines as I moved closer to Silverpine. As much as I liked LA and all it offered, it was no match for the beauty of my hometown. What I hadn't admitted to Caroline or Sophie was that I dreamed about the place often. And in my dreams, I could feel the cool, autumn air against my skin, smell the scent of fresh pines tickling my nose, and hear the birdsong in the trees.

But inevitably that dream would take me to one of two places, both of which left me shaking and upset—I would either hear my mother's voice telling me goodbye for the last time, or I would see the look of betrayal on Jaime's face when I told him I couldn't turn my back on my family.

That look haunted me for twelve years. And I wished I'd found a better way to explain to him back then that turning my back on my family really meant turning my back on my mother. My father made that ultimatum clear. I wasn't worried about leaving behind the Carter fortune—it was the furthest thing from my mind. But I knew with all his power and money, my father would cut me off from my mother, and I knew deep in my bones we needed each other. We were all the other had for many years and I couldn't choose Jaime over her, no matter how much I cared about him.

My anxiety over how I was going to cope with being back at Pine Crest was quickly forgotten because my phone would not stop buzzing.

I'd spent most of the drive to Silverpine on the phone with my father's secretary, Anita. Apparently, what had started as a simple business dinner between Andrew Travers Jr. and I had turned into a formal appreciation event for our most loyal investors. The event would be held in The Lounge at the resort, and the event planners would take care of all the details. I just had to show up and make the rounds.

I didn't understand why the plan changed so dramatically, but Anita explained my father felt if Andrew could see me work my magic with the investors we'd already won over, then it would put him more at ease about the pending merger he had with our company. According to my father, I was to be the belle of the ball and show off like a peacock.

I hated it when he said things like that, and I hated showing off even more. Unlike my father, I treated everyone with respect, when earned, and I often found our clients and investors wanted it better than they gave it. Much to my dismay, my father was a social climber and treated our business as a means to an end. One day, I would be in charge and instill my mother's gentle touch in everything we did. But until then, I'd have to play by his rules.

The upside to the change of plans was that when I arrived at Pine Crest, I wouldn't have time to worry about painful memories. I'd barely stepped out of my rental BMW in the valet line when the head event planner, Linda, hurried toward me from the front entrance, grinning at me broadly. "Miss Carter! We're so delighted to have you home," she said, shaking my hand enthusiastically.

I smiled at her tightly. "Thank you, me, too," I lied.

"I know you must be tired from your drive and all the hard work you've been doing for the company, but Mr.

Carter asked me to get your help ironing out some details about our event tonight before you get too settled in."

I kept a smile pasted on my face. "Of course," I said inwardly, recoiling at the thought.

I hoisted my laptop bag over my shoulder and followed Linda inside the familiar halls of the resort.

It hadn't changed all that much. It was still pristine, the rich wood floors clean as if they'd just been polished that morning, and knowing the standards our management set at the resort, they probably had been. Off to the right was The Lounge, our premier restaurant and bar, where we often held large gatherings and other formal events, and tonight, it would be my little purgatory.

Remember to stay positive, Emma, a voice inside my head that sounded suspiciously like Sophie said.

Something made me pause and stare at the bar, though it wasn't open at that hour. I'd heard through the grapevine Jaime had been working as a bartender for the last several years. From what I'd gathered, he'd developed a reputation as one of the best mixologists that side of the Rockies.

That was no surprise to me. Anything Jaime put his mind to, he excelled at. He was just one of those obnoxiously gifted people.

"Miss Carter?" Linda prompted me.

"What? Oh, I'm sorry, you'll have to forgive me. I'm just a little tired."

"It's understandable. Can I get you something to drink, perhaps some coffee, before we sit down and talk?"

I shook my head, and she led me to a couch in The Lounge, where she filled my ear with details about the event.

When she was done information dumping, I politely excused myself. "I appreciate your help with this Linda, but I need to go up to my room and refresh myself with the Travers' files," I said with a conspiratorial smile. "Showtime will be upon us soon," I said with a wink before hurrying out of there and heading to the family suite.

Unsurprisingly, my bags were already waiting for me.

I spent the next few hours going over the copious amount of notes my father had emailed me about Travers Development, Inc. They were an investment firm out of Florida, and it would appear Mr. Travers Sr. had more money than God. I got worried when I noticed Mr. Travers's acquisitions were mostly land deals. My father had assured me after an argument about the land my mom left to me that he wouldn't press me about developing it, but to be certain, I called him. "Dad, how exactly are we looking to merge with Travers Development? I've read everything in here, but it's not expressly stated."

He paused for a moment before saying, "Well, Mr. Travers deals mostly in land, but he's been looking to diversify his portfolio. I met him skiing a couple of years ago, and I told him if he was ever interested in investing in a resort to remember me, and he did. I've been in contact with him for the last couple of months, but he's nervous about getting into the hospitality game, so we're going to need to hold his hand a little bit."

"I see," I said, my nerves not settled by his answer. But to be fair, I'd been uneasy about most of my father's decisions since my mom died, so I couldn't help but be on high alert.

He'd always loved money, but it alarmed me just how much he loved it. As far as I could tell, it sounded like a standard deal, aside from the fact Travers was new to the hospitality industry. So I could see why my dad was pulling out all the stops to impress them. It was daunting to break into a new industry, no matter how much money and success you had under your belt.

"I think I see what's going on," I said. "Thank you for filling in the gaps. As you know, it helps to have as much information as possible going in."

"Please, my girl, you could sell oceanfront property in the desert. You don't need all this background," he groused, chuckling.

"All the same, Dad, it's nice to know."

"You'll do great, go knock 'em dead."

With those words in my head, I got ready for the evening. What I'd rather do was slip into a pair of yoga pants, my Zac Brown Band t-shirt, and binge on pizza and Netflix. Instead, it would be another long night wearing uncomfortable heels and a slinky dress.

It's not that I didn't enjoy dressing up, but I hadn't slowed down since Mom died, and my body was starting to demand a break.

I was starting to think Caroline and Sophie were right. Once the deal at Pine Crest was done, I needed to insist on a vacation. My strategy of running from the grief over my mother clearly wasn't working, so maybe it was time I took some time to myself. We had several beach resorts I could choose from, and they were calling my name.

I finished curling my hair and putting on finishing touches of makeup, then checked myself out in the mirror. I'd decided on an emerald green metallic dress that hung just above my knees, swishing around my hips but hugging my waist and bust.

My dad had implied I needed to impress Andrew Jr. Though I didn't appreciate the implication, I also wanted the trip to be over as quickly as possible, so if I had to show a little cleavage to expedite the situation, I'd do what needed to be done. I slipped on matching metallic heels, grabbed my clutch, and headed for the elevator, mentally going over my talking points for Andrew and wondering which investors would show up.

When I hit the bottom floor and saw how crowded The Lounge was, a knot of dread wound itself at the bottom of my stomach. I heard raucous laughter coming from the bar, and I turned to look longingly at the bar, which was now open and swinging.

I would love nothing more than to slip into the dim light of the bar and enjoy a vodka tonic—some place where nobody knew me or wanted anything from me.

But that wasn't my assignment for the night. So I turned back to The Lounge and sucked in a deep breath—it was time to go "knock 'em dead."

There was an ache in my face again. Nobody told me that would be a hazard of my job.

I supposed I shouldn't complain. The guests were lovely, and the turnout was better than I'd expected.

Andrew Travers Jr. had yet to show his face, but I had my hands full with the other investors. Many of them had new properties they wanted us to invest in, so they'd offered me a free vacation to check it out. I didn't have the heart to tell them that the last thing I wanted to do was spend my vacation working a deal, especially when so many of those people, while nice enough, could be so damn insufferable. I've never quite gotten over how an investor could treat me so kindly and then bark an order at one of our waitstaff.

I knew how hard the staff worked, and juggling this crowd was no small feat.

After a nasty run-in with a West Coast socialite, I pulled one of the servers aside, "I want to apologize on behalf of that woman."

Even though he looked grateful, he explained, "Oh, don't worry, ma'am, it happens more than you think."

I frowned at him. "That's what I was afraid of. And there's no excuse for it. As soon as I'm done here, I'll make sure you're compensated for the disrespect you've had to put up with."

The server looked even more grateful then. "I really appreciate that, Miss Carter. That's really cool of you. If you need anything at all tonight, just let me know. I'm Joey," he said enthusiastically, sticking out his hand.

"Please, call me Emma. It's nice to meet you, Joey. I think I'm okay for now," I replied.

As he turned to walk away, I realized I might need something a little stronger than my seltzer to get through the night, especially since Andrew Jr. was fashionably late.

"Hey, Joey? On second thought, can you bring me a drink? Something strong enough to help me deal with all these ... lovely people?" I asked with a conspiratorial smile.

Joey smiled. "I'll talk to our mixologist. I'm sure he'll have just the thing."

"Perfect, thank you so much," I said, patting his arm before he dashed off to find a drink that would soothe my frazzled nerves.

Normally, this kind of shindig wouldn't make me so anxious. But having to deal with all these people back at Pine Crest without warning was just too much.

Plus, as time wore on, I was getting increasingly annoyed by the absence of Andrew. I was sure he didn't give a shit, but I was eager to get the deal done so I could get the hell out of here and back to my life in LA.

Joey appeared less than five minutes later with a Collins glass on a tray, looking hopeful. "Ma'am? May I present the Ramos Gin Fizz. Something classic, yet effective … at least that's how they told me to describe it."

I smiled as I took the drink from Joey. "Sounds lovely," I said before taking a sip and letting the smooth cocktail flow down my throat. It was sweet and sour with a creamy finish. "This is excellent," I said as Joey grinned at my satisfaction.

"That's awesome. I'll tell the mixologist. He'll be delighted you like it."

I nodded enthusiastically in agreement. ""Please do. As a matter of fact, I might find him later to thank him personally," I said as Joey looked over my shoulder, his eyes widening slightly.

"Emma?" I turned to see a tall man with blond hair and a grin. He was dressed in a suit and tie, but the tie was loosened, showing a casual attitude for a business meeting. "I'm Andrew Travers," he announced, leaning forward to kiss each of my cheeks.

His move startled me. I was accustomed to the gesture with our European investors, but the Travers' were from the East Coast, and it seemed a little forward on his part, especially after the conversation with my father where he'd suggested Andrew Jr. was a catch.

I took a step back, wanting to make my stance clear. It would be nothing but business. I stuck my hand out to shake his. "Mr. Travers, so nice of you to be here."

"Yeah, sorry I'm a little late. There was a lot more to check out here in Silverpine than I imagined for such a small town. From the way my father described it, I was expecting a dot on the map with a truck stop and a dinky little hotel, but you guys have quite the impressive operation."

Inwardly, I bristled, but outwardly, I kept the smile on my face. "My parents and I have worked very hard to build Pine Crest Mountain Resort into what it is today. We're extremely proud, and I think once you experience it for yourself, you'll understand why."

Andrew looked down at me suggestively. "I'm sure I will," he said with a cocked brow.

I suppressed an eye roll and took another step back. "Why don't we get you something to drink and go over some of the details our fathers have negotiated?"

"Oh, let's not ruin this amazing party with business. We can save that for the dinner we're supposed to have. I'd rather get to know you, Emma," he said, his eyes sweeping to the low neckline of my dress, and suddenly, the idea I could close the deal quicker with cleavage felt a little ickier than it had a few hours ago.

"Well," I said cautiously, trying to regain my composure, "you said you looked around Silverpine today, so chances are you've gotten to know me already just by being here." I then proceeded to tell him about where I went to high school and give him some history about my mother's family and the land Pine Crest sat on. We discussed where I went to business school and how I worked my way up to become my father's right hand—anything to distract him from the personal stuff. I was hoping he'd pick up the hint, and we could get back to business.

While I appreciated my business colleagues being straight to the point, there was a forwardness about Andrew that rubbed me the wrong way. Or perhaps I was being overly sensitive because of where we were. I didn't have my typical business shield up. Sometimes it felt like I was walking around with one big raw open wound.

Which was why I needed to keep my eye on the prize and remember my beach vacation. The sooner I got the business done, the quicker I could get on to the business of healing.

As luck would have it, one of the other investors recognized Andrew and joined our conversation, giving me a buffer, which I was grateful for. Over the next couple hours, guests started saying their goodbyes, moving on to other parties or just going to their rooms, and I graciously bid them adieu, counting down the minutes until I too could escape.

Andrew talked about damn near everything other than business, and I would soon learn it wasn't difficult to change the subject. As long as I steered the conversation toward him, he would run with it.

I heard all about his jet setting, his wannabe athletic exploits, and how he was finally joining the family business to help "dear old dad," as he put it.

I'd done my research before the night's event, and I knew a little about Andrew Sr., but his son made him sound like a doddering old fool, which didn't match the impression I got. As far as I could tell, his father was a rather robust and calculated businessman.

It amused me that a grown man lacked the maturity to appreciate the success of his father when it was painfully obvious he struggled to measure up. And it made Andrew Jr. even less attractive than I'd originally thought.

He was in the middle of outlining all the outdoor adventures he had planned while he in Silverpine when I realized I'd been lost in my own thoughts, and unsurprisingly, Andrew hadn't noticed.

"That sounds wonderful," I said, trying to grasp onto anything we had in common. "I used to hike these mountains regularly with my mom when she was still alive. It's beautiful country."

Andrew looked a little odd for a second, then grinned at me. "Indeed, it is, but sometimes we have to make sacrifices so others can enjoy it."

I felt an icy prick in my gut. "They're here for everybody to enjoy. I believe land should largely be left alone. It seems everything needs to be profited on. Nothing is sacred. I mean, do we really need another mini mall?" I asked, laughing.

Another odd expression crossed Andrew's face, but then he laughed it off. Thankfully, I was saved from any more awkward conversations when the last of the guests approached me to say their goodnights. I used it as an opportunity to address Andrew, too, and said, "Well, if you'll excuse me, it's been a really long day, so I'm going to head back to my room now. I'm sure you'll want to be well rested for your excursions tomorrow, too."

He nodded in agreement. "It was *really* nice meeting you, Emma," he said, and I tried to ignore the churn I felt in my stomach.

"Are we still on for dinner tomorrow to review the nuts and bolts of the operation?" I asked, trying to steer it back to the reason we were there in the first place.

He nodded. "I will be there—on time, of course," he said with a grin.

I told him goodnight and watched until he'd exited the restaurant before turning to the remaining wait staff and announcing, "Alright, guys, you were outstanding tonight. I'm going to make sure everyone gets an extra twenty percent tip tonight. I cannot thank you enough for this evening."

After the servers said their thanks and told me goodnight, I marched through The Lounge toward the elevator before stopping short, my eyes catching on the bar.

After the long evening I had, I could really go for another Gin Fizz. And I completely forgot I wanted to thank the mixologist myself and tell them how much I appreciated the drink.

Even though I was dead on my feet and wanted nothing more than to get out of these stupid heels, I changed course and stepped into the dim bar.

Even though there were still a few hours until last call, only a few tables were occupied. It was quiet, which I was grateful for.

I would enjoy a quick drink, then hit the hay. However, when I approached the bar, it was noticeably empty. I looked around for a bartender and found none. Maybe they were in back room restocking?

I sat on a stool and, as I waited, surveyed the place. It had changed since I'd last saw it—the liquor bottles were now displayed on illuminated stair-stepped platforms be-hind the bar, and the abstract wall art gave it a more modern feel. It may be a mountain resort, but the bar felt sexy, and I liked it.

My father never saw the point in spending money on the resort's bar decor because he believed that as long as there was alcohol, the guests would come. I'd heard there was a new manager and mixologist hired recently and wondered if it was their handiwork. It would appear I had two compliments to deliver … if only I could find that bartender.

Just then I heard a shuffling behind me and turned, expecting to find the bartender when the breath got knocked out of me.

"Jaime," I breathed, coming face to face with my sexy ghost for the first time in twelve years.

Jaime

It had been incredibly busy for a weeknight. My staff and I had run our asses off trying to keep up with the event in The Lounge.

The guests were extra demanding, and I even caught a few of the servers tearing up after some particularly cruel comments. But whoever oversaw the event was apparently quite nice and promised them a generous tip, so the staff soldiered on, and I kept encouraging them we would get through it.

I'd soon learn it was some corporate event hosted by the resort, and I couldn't help but wonder if Emma ever went to those things.

Who was I kidding? Of course, she did. I knew she had to rub elbows with those kinds of pricks all the time, and she probably did so with ease.

That was just her way. She could always talk to anybody. I wished for that ability with some of my servers after the night we had, but the best I could give them was, "We'll get through this."

As I saw the guests file out of The Lounge at a faster pace, I breathed a sigh of relief. The wait staff would be busy cleaning it up while the rest of the bar staff would finally have time to restock. Despite their entitled natures, the guests made us a lot of money, so I guess I couldn't complain too much.

I spent the last half hour in my office tallying the evening's totals and closing out the books while the bar staff wiped down tables and restocked. Once they were finished, I sent them into The Lounge to help the other waitstaff clean up after the party. No one wanted to be there any longer than necessary.

I leaned back in my chair to peek out my office door and spotted a sexy redhead.

"Get a hold of yourself," I scolded myself. "It's probably the same woman as before."

After the last redheaded spotting, when I embarrassed myself in front of Charlie, I vowed to not let Emma Carter mess with my head any longer.

But then I saw all the staff was gone, and no one was behind the bar to help the guest. So I jumped up and made my way behind the bar. As I opened my mouth to speak, everything stood still for one heart-stopping moment.

A beautiful, heart-shaped face turned toward me and her red-painted bow mouth dropped into an "o" shape before it breathed out one word, "Jaime?"

Well, I'll be damned. After nearly giving myself whiplash, turning to glimpse every redhead who crossed my path, hoping it might be Emma, she finally appeared like some heavenly angel dropped in the middle of my bar.

"Emma?" I said, my voice sounding rusty.

I cleared my throat and started again. "You're here. I mean, of course, you're here. It's your resort. What I meant was, what brings you back?" I asked.

She gave me a gracious smile. "The resort was hosting an event for investors at The Lounge tonight," she said, pointing unnecessarily over her shoulder.

"I should've guessed you would have something to do with that."

She laughed. "I can understand why you would be surprised considered I haven't been back to Silverpine since …" She trailed off, looking away, and then turned to face me again. "Since my mom died."

I was struck by how much she resembled the Emma I knew, and yet she'd grown into a beautiful, successful woman I knew nothing about—it was a strange feeling.

She'd filled out since the last time I'd seen her, and her womanly curves made my cock stir behind my zipper.

But there was something darker in her eyes, a sadness that didn't used to be there.

"I heard about Lydia. I'm so sorry, Emma. I know how close you two were."

She swallowed hard. "Thank you, Jaime," and then asked, "So, you're working here now?"

I nodded. "Yeah, I know it's crazy, but it's the best paying gig in town."

She shook her head. "I knew they'd hired a new mixologist, but I had no idea …" she said, trailing off again.

"Is that a problem for you?" I couldn't help but ask although I immediately regretted it.

"Oh, no," she rushed to say, laughing, embarrassed. "I'm just surprised. It's been such a long time." She glanced away again before pressing forward with a determined set to her shoulders. That was the Emma I remembered. She would never let a situation stay awkward for too long.

"I wanted to talk to the head mixologist to compliment him."

I grinned stupidly at her. Goddamn, I felt like a kid talking to her, not a grown man having a conversation with another adult.

Except she wasn't just any adult. It was the woman who'd turned my world upside down, who'd haunted my every move for over a decade.

"I asked the server, Joey, for a drink to help me get through the evening, and you delivered. Were you the one who made the Gin Fizz?"

I nodded, remembering that specific request from Joey. "Yep, that was me," I said proudly.

She beamed at me. "It was perfect. I mean it. I don't know why it's such a hard one for bartenders to get, but it was just perfect and exactly what I needed."

I nodded in understanding. "Rough crowd tonight?"

She laughed, shaking her head. "Hardly rough, but … I don't know. I just wasn't in the right headspace to deal with them tonight; I needed a little extra liquid courage, I guess. And your staff was wonderful. I know those folks aren't always the easiest to deal with, and they were so professional and good to them."

"Good, I'll pass it on to my team tomorrow. I know they'll appreciate the compliments."

I couldn't believe what was happening. Emma Carter was standing right in front of me. I could literally reach out and touch her—and there was absolutely nothing I wanted to do more.

There was another strained silence before she cleared her throat and asked point blank, "What are you doing back in Silverpine? I mean, I got the impression you didn't want to come back here ever again the last time I saw you," she said hastily.

"Your impression would be correct," I said, chuckling. "I'm back because of Mom. She's been battling dementia for a while now, and over the last few months, it's gotten worse. We have in-home care for her now."

"Oh, Jaime, I'm so sorry to hear that."

I nodded and thanked her. "It's been rough. It's hard to watch her slowly disappear. She was such a force."

"I can understand that. Imagining Esmeralda as anything other than the fierce mama bear I knew must be challenging. How are the girls handling it?" she asked, referring to my sisters, Silvia and Maria.

"It's been difficult for everyone. Silvia keeps her distance. Her and Mom had a falling out, so it's been awkward, but she tries to help in her own way, just quietly and behind the scenes. Maria practically lives there, but that will have to change when the baby arrives."

Emma's eyebrows shot up. "Maria is having a baby?"

I nodded. "Yeah, I know. It's hard for me to wrap my head around, too. When she told me I had to resist the urge to knock her husband's teeth out. He's a good guy though, and they're happy."

"I guess a lot has changed since the last time I saw you," she whispered, and there was that sadness again.

I smiled at her. "It's been twelve years, Emma," I reminded her.

"Yeah," she breathed, sadness overtaking her once more.

All I wanted to do was jump over the bar and pull her into my arms—to comfort her and take her sadness away. But that wouldn't be appropriate considering the circumstances, and I wasn't even sure she'd welcome the gesture.

I tore my gaze away from her and busied my hands wiping down an already immaculate bar with my towel.

"So, how does it feel to be back? I'm guessing you stayed away because of her?" I probably shouldn't have asked that question, but I never had much of a filter, and that was something Emma used to love about me—I hoped that hadn't changed.

She gave a small smile and nodded, swallowing hard before saying, "Yeah, everything here reminds me of her. Which isn't a bad thing, but it's just …"

"Tough."

"Yeah," she breathed. "But the show must go on as my dad likes to say," she remarked, and I had to rein in my response at the mention of her father.

"Hmm, and how is dear old dad these days?" I asked, hoping to God my tone was casual enough and didn't give away the vitriol and distaste I still felt for the man.

If it did, Emma was too polite to acknowledge it because she just smiled, seemingly grateful for a topic other than her late mother. "He's the same old cantankerous man. Hasn't slowed down a bit. If anything, he's more determined than ever to conquer the world."

I couldn't help but notice the tinge of worry in Emma's voice when she described her father. Though it didn't surprise me one bit John Carter had only grown more determined in his goal of world domination. Mrs. Carter always seemed to keep him in line, but with her gone, I doubted anyone could get through to him now, not even Emma.

Emma sighed and refocused her gaze on me. "No more dwelling on the sad stuff. I want to hear about you. Where have you been since you left Silverpine? Tell me everything."

Though I couldn't blame her for changing the subject, it made me sad. The old Emma didn't feel uncomfortable in raw moments. She sat with her feelings and dealt with them head-on, but I couldn't fault her for protecting herself, not after everything she'd gone through. I just never thought she would put up a shield with me.

I tried not to let that fact dishearten me as I regaled her with stories of all the places I'd been and where I'd worked over the last decade. I didn't take the easiest path in life, but it had allowed me to explore much of the country and meet a lot of interesting people.

I told her about my years in Texas, serving fancy drinks to high rollers at the rodeos and how, at the end of the shows, I'd go out to the barns with a bottle of whiskey for the bull riders because if anybody needed a drink, it was guys who'd just risked their lives. I told her about my time up in the Pacific Northwest, where I spent most of my time in cities like Portland and Seattle making funky concoctions for the Gen X crowd and giving them goofy names like "Tastes Like Teen Spirits" or the "Ice, Ice Baby" followed by a "No Scrubs" chaser.

It was heaven on earth to hear her laugh again. A part of me was convinced I would never hear it again even as the rest of me hoped that wouldn't be true.

She sat across from me, entertained by my stories as she sipped on another Gin Fizz I'd prepared for her. Those emerald eyes were focused on me like I was the only person in the room, and it all came rushing back. How she had a talent for making anyone feel special just by focusing all her attention on them. But it didn't feel like a business maneuver. It was just Emma. Sweet, thoughtful … seductive Emma. She had no idea how crazy she still made me by just sitting perched on that stool, leaning forward and smiling warmly at me—while the low neckline of her shimmery dress revealed soft cleavage that taunted me. I'd fantasized about those curves a lot over the years, more than I cared to admit.

Still, it was as if someone plugged me in as I leaned across the bar all relaxed and delighted her with story after story of my adventures. Of course, I left out the part where I missed her and wished I could have shared every one of them with her. How everything reminded me of her and how, at the end of each day, I ached to tell her about everything that had happened. How sometimes I did anyway, alone in the dark, whispering to the walls like I was talking to her.

It was the echo of those conversations that always made me feel the loneliest. But not tonight. Tonight, Emma Carter was sitting inches away from me, laughing, smiling, and asking questions about what life without her was like. Of course, she didn't word it that way. She asked me what I'd been up to, all the places I'd seen and the things I'd learned. She didn't need to know everything I'd done in the last twelve years was filed under the banner of "Life Without Emma."

I wasn't about to share that, especially because she made her choice a long time ago. There was no point in making her feel guilty about it now … even though I still had so many questions.

She was laughing at another of my stories when Joey hesitantly tapped me on the shoulder. I turned to him in surprise. I'd forgotten there was anybody else here, but then I glanced out into the dining room and saw all the guests had gone. "Sorry to interrupt, boss, but it's closing time," Joey said.

"Oh, my goodness, I hadn't realized it had gotten so late," Emma said. "I should get out of your hair."

"No," I said a little too forcefully. I laughed it off, but out of the corner of my eye, I saw Joey eyeing me strangely before melting back into the background. "I mean, you weren't in my hair … It's been really good to see you, Emma. You can crash my shift anytime," I said, wondering if I was laying it on too thick, but my worry was extinguished when she smiled at me.

"It's been good to see you, too, Jaime. I was really dreading coming back to Pine Crest, but now, I'm thinking it might not be so bad," she said with a mischievous glint in her eye.

I bit my lip, trying to hold back my grin and failing. "How long are you back?"

She let out a long sigh. "I'm not sure. My dad has me here to broker some deal he's been quite ambiguous about, so I should know more tomorrow. Maybe you and I can steal some time away later and catch up properly?" she asked, and it might have been my imagination, but there was a suggestion of something more in her voice.

"Yeah, that would be great," I answered much too quickly; though I noticed she didn't mind my eagerness. My God, it felt like nothing had changed. She was just as receptive to me now as she was back then. We were kids then. Could we just pick up where we'd left off?

"Good," she smiled. "I have some business to tend to tomorrow night, but maybe afterward, I can swing by, and we can make plans?"

"I'll be here," I answered.

She slipped from the stool and grabbed her clutch, holding my eyes the whole time. "I'll see you tomorrow," she said, reaching out and touching my hand. The touch was brief and light, but I felt a surge of electricity rush through my body.

She must have felt it, too, because her eyes immediately found mine as she pulled her hand away. Even in the dim light of the bar, I could see the deep blush creeping up her beautiful pale skin.

Clearing her throat and taking a step back, "Goodnight, Jaime," she murmured, her voice barely above a whisper.

There was a tightness in my chest I hadn't felt in far too long. "Goodnight, Emma," I answered gruffly. I was fairly certain there wasn't a drop of blood actually making it to my brain as every bit had rushed to my dick. I'd never been so grateful to have a bar in between us. Otherwise, I would have thoroughly embarrassed myself.

She smiled and turned to leave. As she walked toward the exit, the light from the lobby silhouetted her figure, and I couldn't decide if it made her look like an angel or vixen.

But when she turned one last time, making eye contact with me over her shoulder, giving me a small wave before stepping out of sight, I decided she was definitely more vixen.

And just like that, Emma Carter was back, and I knew with certainty I was in serious trouble … and I couldn't wait to enjoy every minute.

Emma

I didn't remember getting on the elevator or walking down the hallway toward my room. I just remembered the overwhelming rush of heat and disbelief that I had just reconnected with Jaime Acosta.

What were the odds we'd be here at the same time? Hell, what were the odds he'd be working at the resort? That in itself felt like hell freezing over, considering the hatred I knew he felt toward my father. There was definitely no love lost between the two men, especially after my father forbade me from seeing "that boy." I still remember the way he spit out those words, as if Jaime was a pesky insect who needed to be squashed.

I stopped short of my door, leaning against the wall because it felt like the world was spinning. Maybe it was the Gin Fizz … or more likely, the man who prepared them.

The whole evening blew my mind. We'd slipped into conversation with one another as if the last time we'd spoken was mere hours before and not more than a decade ago. And yet … there was something new there.

There was no denying I'd been sexually attracted to Jaime when we were younger. He was tall, dark, and handsome—but he was also smart and so interesting to talk to. I'd loved his stories. He could spin a yarn out of something as simple as a trip to the gas station. Obviously, that hadn't changed.

What had changed was that tall, dark, and handsome Jaime Acosta had filled out. Those wide shoulders I'd loved when we were younger also had impressive musculature attached to them. Those dark, sexy eyes had picked up some experience along the way, and it showed in the way they'd quickly assessed me. The way his eyes lingered across my chest could have offended me, but then his eyes also lingered on mine as if they were searching for something. Being studied like that made me feel vulnerable, but it also felt like the first time I'd been truly seen in a very long time.

The memory of it made my skin prickle, along with the realization that Jaime now had a deep, sexy voice that rolled down my spine and caused sensations in my core unlike anything I'd ever felt.

It was all just too much. What the hell was I doing making plans to see him again? It could only end in heartbreak.

The last few days had been a whirlwind, and I needed a good night's sleep. Only then could I figure my next steps.

But first, I needed to get myself off the wall. Too bad it was the only thing holding me up at the moment, and even though I wanted to blame the Gin Fizz, something in me knew it was simply the Jaime Effect. I never would have imagined he'd still have that kind of impact on me after all these years.

Sucking in a deep breath, I straightened and faced my door, fumbling with my key as I unlocked it. Opening the door, I nearly screamed in shock when Caroline emerged from around the corner, smiling sheepishly. "Surprise!"

It took me a moment to process what was going on, and that was when Caroline approached me, looking concerned. "Oh, no, I should've called first. That was dumb of me. I didn't even consider you've probably had more than enough surprises over the last few days."

I looked at her in disbelief, a stupefied smile overtaking my mouth. "You have no idea."

An hour later, Caroline and I were both in our jammies, devouring room service cheeseburgers and fries while I filled her in on my unexpected reunion of the night.

"So, tell me. What was it *really* like—seeing him again?" she asked, delight in her eyes.

"It was … nice," I finished lamely.

Caroline rolled her eyes. "Emma, come on. It's me."

I averted my eyes. "What?" I insisted, shrugging indifferently.

"Oh, you are so full of it. It was nice? You've been carrying a torch for this guy for twelve years. That either means you have a really unhealthy attachment, or he's really that amazing. Now you've seen him in the flesh and talked to him for over an hour, was he worth pining over for all these years?"

I pursed my lips together in displeasure. That was what I both loved and hated about Caroline—she didn't pull any punches. Right about now seemed like a good time to entertain my denial, but I knew she wouldn't let me get away with it. "Who said I was pining after him?"

Caroline snickered, pausing in between bites. "Please, Emma. I have eyes and ears and know you better than anyone. You can play coy all you want, but you came in here all hot and bothered after your rendezvous. And while I realize my schlubby travel attire of yoga pants and t-shirt is knuckle-bitingly sexy, I don't think it was me who caused that flush in your cheeks."

I let out a long sigh, pausing before finally admitting, "It was like no time had passed. We could always talk for hours, sometimes about nothing at all, and still have fun together."

"A man you can talk to? Wow," Caroline muttered sarcastically.

"Yeah, but it wasn't just that, Caroline. I mean, I've always thought he was hot, but tonight, there was something else I can't really explain. It was new and unbridled and like …" I trailed off, struggling to come up with the proper explanation.

"Like you wanted to rip each other's clothes off and have hot animal sex on the bar?" Caroline offered.

My eyes widened, and I felt my cheeks flush.

"Well?" Caroline pressed.

"Yeah," I whispered. "How did you know?"

Caroline laughed. "An educated guess. Think about it, Emma. You two were practically babies when you last saw each other, and while you were drawn to him then, there's a very big difference between teenage boy cute and grown man hot. Young men are excited about the possibility of seeing someone naked. Grown ass men look at you in a way that lets you know they have very specific plans for what they want to do to you …"

Leave it to Caroline to break down a sensually palpable moment to that of textbook science.

"So, my next question is … did Mr. Acosta look at you like he had plans for you?"

My mind rushed back to the memory of Jaime's eyes skating all over me and how they'd returned to my gaze with a fresh heat. Did he have plans for me? The mere thought of it made me feel hot all over again.

"Aaaand, I will take that dreamy expression on your face as a yes," Caroline said, smiling.

I warmed even more beneath her speculative gaze. "I haven't told you everything … I made plans to see him again."

Her eyes widened, and a mischievous smile stole over her lips. "Oh, I see. Arranging a little bump and grind time. Alright, Carter, that's what I'm talking about."

My head shook in denial before she'd even finished speaking. "No, no, no, nothing like that."

Caroline looked at me sternly. "And why not?"

My heart raced at the possibility, even as my mind insisted it was not an option. "Because …" I started, my mouth searching for the right words. Caroline watched me impatiently with raised eyebrows. Finally, I huffed out, "it's complicated."

"Ah, yes, the old standby. Well, my dear, the solution is simple—uncomplicate it."

"That's easy for you to say. You haven't been living with the pain of having to choose between family and Jaime."

"True. But the fact is, you're adults. You could have a mutually satisfying affair while you're here as long as you both understand what the boundaries are."

"Boundaries?" I squeaked out.

"I'm not talking about coming up with a safe word—although that could be fun. I'm just saying if you know this is just sex while you're here, then that needs to be communicated up front. That way, you might actually have some fun on this God forsaken trip," she clarified.

The thought was intriguing, but … "It's hard to think about Jaime as just sex, though."

Caroline snickered. "Please, if you ask me, that's the only way to think about any man. They're too much trouble otherwise."

I grimaced at her declaration, but I wasn't surprised. Caroline had grown up as a child of divorce with parents. She didn't have the rosiest outlook on relationships, and she'd proclaimed more than once the idea of a "one true love" was a crock of shit.

While I disagreed with her, it was not the moment to have a philosophical debate about love.

"When are you going to see him again?"

"I don't know. Maybe I shouldn't," I mumbled.

"Come on, Emma, you have to see him. Even if you don't get physical, you know you'll regret it if you don't. As long as I've known you, you've wondered about this guy. Maybe if you spend some time with him, you can at least get some closure."

"Maybe," I said, my mind twisting it over. "God, Caroline. I'm so sorry. I've been going on and on about myself, and I haven't even asked what possessed you to come here? I thought you were chained to your desk for the foreseeable future?"

Caroline's expression dropped for a moment before she pasted a bright, very un-Caroline smile onto her face. "Well, you and Sophie keep saying I need a vacation."

"Yeah, but we've been saying that forever. Why would you take our advice now?" I asked, observing her carefully. Caroline could be cagey, and out of the three of us, she was definitely the most mysterious. I never got the impression she did it intentionally, though. She just played her cards close to the vest even with her best friends.

I could see the wheels spinning in her head, but I kept my steady gaze on her, hoping if I stayed unwavering, she would fold.

She held eye contact for a long moment before finally huffing out a dramatic sigh and saying, "Fine, but I don't want you telling Sophie yet. I love her, but I'm not in the mood to hear her sunshine and rainbows take on it."

I nodded. "You have my word. Now tell me what happened."

Her shoulders slumped in defeat before she said, "That promotion I've been busting my ass over? The one that's had me practically living in the office? They gave it to Gerard—the guy I just got done training a couple months ago."

"Are you kidding? Why on earth did they give it to that guy? He couldn't possibly have outperformed everyone else in such a short amount of time. Not to mention you've been there way longer."

I knew all about Caroline's trainee. She'd agreed to take on training him, even though she didn't have the capacity with her workload. But she was told it would look great to the powers that be who handed out promotions. Now, Gerard had usurped her, and all her hard work had been for nothing.

Caroline shook her head. "Apparently, he has one quality I don't possess—an uncle who works in HR."

"That's bullshit."

"You're telling me. When they made the announcement, the other candidates just let it roll off their backs, even though I knew they were seething. But I couldn't fake it anymore. I went to my supervisor and told him how I felt, and he said 'I would have to try a little harder next time.'"

I let out a squawk. "That's ridiculous. You work everyone under the table. That place wouldn't still be standing if it wasn't for you."

She sighed, staring out the window. "I love you for saying that, but unfortunately, they don't see it that way."

"So, what happened? Did you quit? No one would blame you for walking out of there."

She smiled at me ruefully. "I wish I could tell you I stormed out of there in a blaze of glory. But once I got done shadow boxing in the women's restroom, I marched into HR and told them I needed a mental health vacation effective immediately. Since I'd yet to take off a single day this year, not even when I was sick, they didn't fight me … That or they saw the unhinged look in my eyes and decided not to push the issue."

I reached across the loveseat and pulled her into my arms. She was stiff at first, typical Caroline, but it didn't take long for her to sag against me, and then the tears started. She was always so hard on herself.

"I'm sorry," she sobbed. "You're going through all this big stuff being back here, and I'm crying like a baby over a stupid job."

"No, it's not stupid. I know how much this meant to you."

"I didn't know where to go, and I couldn't stomach the idea of holing up in my apartment wallowing. Plus, I was worried about you. It was really shitty of your dad to put you in this position," she insisted. "The next thing I knew, I was on the next flight to Denver."

I pulled back, smoothing back her ruffled hair. "Well, I'm thrilled you're here. Even if the reason sucks. Now that you're here, your assignment is to relax and not think about those assholes back in LA."

"Yeah, right," she snorted, "I have to figure out how I'm going to walk back in there after my outburst."

I raised an irritated eyebrow. "I've been asking you to come work for us for ages, but you have to be stubborn."

Caroline sniffed. "The last thing I want is to become a nepotism hire. I know I'm all blubbery now, but I don't want you to worry. I'll figure something out. You may be right about one thing, though …"

"What are you talking about? I'm right about a ton of things."

She rolled her eyes. "Ha, ha. It'll be good for me to think about something other than work for a while. And lucky for me, now I get to think about what *you* have going on …" she mused.

I huffed out a laugh. "All I have going on," I said, gliding off the loveseat and busying my hands with unpacking my suitcase, "is nailing down this deal for my father."

"And you know … nailing the hot bartender," Caroline interjected.

I snatched a pillow off the bed and chucked it at her, shaking my head at her cackle. I was so grateful she was here. Maybe the presence of an unexpected roommate would help me control myself around Jaime though I suspected that would be a tall order.

Jaime

♥

Getting home that night was a blur. I was grateful it was late on a weeknight, and nobody was on the road because I remembered little about the drive other than it felt like I was floating.

"C'mon, man. Get your shit together," I muttered as I turned onto the familiar street and drove toward my childhood home. It was odd to return home as an adult to live in your parent's house. I had so many fond memories of growing up in that house … and spending time with Emma. *My Emma.*

The words sounded in my head before I could stop them. She wasn't *my Emma*, I had to remind myself. We were thirty years old and had lived completely different lives. Still, after spending just an hour basking in her light, I was already pawing at the ground, claiming her as mine once again.

It wasn't outside the realm of possibility … She wanted to see me again. And I noticed the flush in her cheeks when I not so subtly studied the curves of her body while we spoke. A thread of giddiness raced through me, and I felt like a kid again—until I pulled into the driveway of my mother's house.

Ever since her diagnosis, there was a sense of melancholy whenever I stepped inside. Our roles were reversed now, my sister and I caring for her with the help of an in-home caregiver.

The nurse was great and worked her ass off. We really appreciated everything she was doing for our mom. But it was unnerving having a stranger in the house caring for your formerly fiercely independent mother. My father used to joke it wasn't worth it to say "bless you" to my mother when she sneezed because she would take offense and respond with "What? You think I need your help with blessings?"

To make matters worse, I never knew what I was walking into—whether Ma was having a good or bad day, if she was present, or living in a different decade. It was stressful to experience as a child, but I could only imagine how disorienting it was for her being corrected on little things like the date or what her husband's name was.

When I pulled into the driveway, I noticed it wasn't the little sedan the nurse usually drove but Maria's truck. Worried, I hurried into the house to find my little sister sitting on the couch, watching a late-night comedian, a tangle of knitting in her hands concealing her growing belly.

"You haven't given up on that mess yet?" I asked her, nodding my head to the pink mass of yarn piled on her stomach.

"Mama didn't raise no quitter. Besides, she knitted a receiving blanket for every one of us, and I'm going to carry on that tradition for this little one," she said, not bothering to look up from her project, her brows furrowed in concentration. "I just wish Mama remembered she knows how to do this so she could show me how."

That statement struck a chord, but I pushed the pang down. "What are you doing here, anyway? What happened to Sheila?" I asked, referring to the nurse.

"Her daughter spiked a fever, so she had to leave early," Maria explained.

"What about Silvia? You should get your rest before that baby gets here," I told her as if she actually needed reminding.

"Why bother Silvia with this? It's not like I'm going to be sleeping anyway. As big as this baby's getting, I can't get into any position that's comfortable. At least here I can help and be productive," Maria said, ever pragmatic.

"Hmm," I grunted. "How is Ma tonight?" I asked, fortifying myself for the answer.

"She was fairly peaceful tonight. She thought I was a neighbor girl in the village, so I heard a lot of village gossip—forty years after the fact—but it made for an enjoyable evening."

I smiled. As practical as Maria was, she still put a positive light on just about everything. I envied her.

"What about you? How was it at the bar tonight?" she asked, looking up from her knitting.

"Not bad. Had an event with a bunch of high rollers that kept us busy, but we got through it. The staff earned extra tips from it. Oh, and I ran into Emma. So, overall, not a bad night," I said casually, plopping down on the couch next to Maria and idly picking at the basket of spare yarn in between us.

Maria wasn't falling for any casual turn of phrase, and she looked at me through narrowed eyes. "I'm sorry, did you say Emma?"

"Yeah," I shrugged, regretting mentioning her at all. I couldn't mention someone as important as Emma without my sisters following the scent like bloodhounds. Subtlety was not their strong suit.

"As in Emma Carter?" she clarified, a grin wreathing her mouth.

I glanced at her, then turned away to work on getting my boots off. "Yeah, what's the big deal?" I asked, managing to do it with a straight face.

"What's the big deal? Are you serious right now?" Maria asked incredulously, dropping her knitting and turning to face me on the couch. I was in for it now though I didn't mind. It wasn't like I could talk to Charlie about Emma. He'd have nothing but dire warnings.

"You're telling me the woman you've been longing for since you were a teenager, the one who got away with your heart, the one you look for around every corner … just drops into your bar, and that's no big deal?"

I rolled my eyes. "That's a little dramatic, don't you think?"

She huffed. "No, I don't think it is. It's romantic … and tragic but mostly romantic. I mean, missing someone for that long? I can't even imagine."

"Yeah, well, that's because Carlos was smart enough to know a good thing when he found it and stuck to you like glue," I teased her.

Maria smiled, petting her bulging belly. It was a little gag worthy to see her so swoony over Carlos like she was still a teenager. But it was also comforting to know that even though she and Carlos had been together for several years, they still acted like lovesick kids around one another. I was happy my little sister had that. If only we were all so lucky.

I tried to ignore the pang of envy in my chest. It never seemed to matter how many years passed or all the reasons Emma left. I still felt like we'd been robbed of something. The reminder made me stiffen my posture. Shaking my head, I told Maria, "That was a million years ago. It's probably best to leave the past in the past, don't you think?"

Maria didn't answer right away, contemplating me with her head tilted to the side. Finally, she said, "Tell me this, Jaime. When you saw her again, what was your first reaction?"

Excitement. Lust. Longing … Relief.

I cleared my throat. "It's been a long night, Maria," I said as I shuffled off the couch and gathered up my boots. "I should go to bed."

Maria raised a dubious eyebrow. "You can avoid telling me the truth all you want, Jaime, but don't make the mistake of lying to yourself. That only leads to trouble."

I stopped in the doorway, not bothering to look back. "You know, you're really starting to sound like Mom."

I didn't catch her expression as I headed for the stairs, but I heard her little gasp and then a quiet and sincere "Thanks." I bit back a laugh. If I'd said the same thing to my oldest sister Silvia, she would have thrown a chancla at my head. But to Maria, there was no greater compliment.

I shook my head as I headed up the stairs, the events of the day finally catching up to my body. I guess the adrenaline was wearing off. Although she was the baby of the family, Maria really was wise beyond her years. And her question continued to ring through my ears as I grabbed my pajama pants and headed to the shower.

So many emotions collided within me when I laid eyes on Emma. It was exhilarating … and absolutely terrifying, especially the feeling of relief that washed over me. I was aware of how hard it had been to live without her all this time, but this was the first time I realized I'd been holding my breath for years.

With Emma back in Silverpine, I could breathe again. The oxygen was rushing through my bloodstream, and while I wanted to drink in the air and fill my lungs, there was a real possibility the feeling wouldn't last. She would probably only be here for a few days, and then what? I would be right back where I started—maybe even worse.

The fact of the matter was another taste of Emma could end me.

And yet I knew with the clarity of a man walking toward his executioner, there was no going back.

If she were to offer herself up, I would go all in like a man diving into his last meal, and I would savor every bite. And as I stood beneath the warm spray of my shower, I let my imagination run wild, thinking about how heavenly Emma would taste. How she would respond in my arms, throwing her head back and revealing the milky, sensitive skin of her neck.

Then I thought about my fingers tracing the low neckline of that dress, my lips following in their wake and how I'd slip the thin straps off her shoulders and let the shimmery mass fall to the floor.

Emma had always been a stunner. My beam of light with that dazzling smile. But now that she'd grown into those beautiful curves, and after watching the enticing sway of her generous hips as she walked away from me, it took everything in me not to hop over the bar and hunt her down.

I wondered how she would've reacted if I had. If I'd grabbed her and backed her into the wall of the lobby and taken her mouth, claiming her out in the open for anyone to see.

My hand tightened around my shaft, and my strokes became more aggressive at the image. Would her creamy, fair skin blush at my touch? Starting high in her cheeks, running all the way down to her breasts?

That was all it took to inspire my release. I was needy for her. The mere thought of a blush was enough to make me come hard in my hand, breathing hard in the shower until I came back to my senses and remembered where the hell I was. I let the hot water wash over me for a little while longer and then forced myself to turn it off and dry off.

She'd only been back for a few hours, and I was already wrestling with myself, torn over what to do.

I glimpsed myself in the mostly steamed over mirror and laughed. Who was I kidding? I knew exactly what I was going to do … I was going to take any and every opportunity to get close to her again even though it might wind up hurting like hell. But it would be worth it.

Emma

I certainly didn't expect to be up as early as I was. Then again, everything about the last few days had been unexpected. Between the excitement of running into Jaime and staying up late with Caroline, I fully expected to sleep like the dead, but here I was at the mahogany secretary's desk going over financials for *Get Outdoors*, the Travers' outdoor sports tour business.

I could still hear Caroline snoring softly from the bedroom as I focused on the figures before me like my life depended on it though it was futile because all I could think about was Jaime.

I still couldn't get over running into him here, of all places. Pine Crest had been a big bone of contention for us back in the day. I worried he'd believed I was just doing my father's bidding by choosing my family over him. But the resort was important to me—not because of the money it made my family but because of what it meant to my mom and the way it had supported the local community since it was built thirty years ago.

Silverpine was still a small town, thanks to our elected officials. They'd refused permits to big box stores and limited development of strip malls. The vacationers who came in droves to the resort had no choice but to frequent the small family-run businesses and boutique shops. I was proud of that. The resort helped fuel the community my mother had spent her life adoring and serving.

I'd been terrified to lose Jaime back then but was even more fearful of losing my mother, and now here I was without either of them. At least I'd gotten those final few years with my mom. It made me think about Jaime's mom, Esmeralda. She'd always been such a spitfire. Her not remembering her past or her children tore at me. I could only imagine how difficult it was for Jaime, Silvia, and Maria to watch her slowly decline.

I felt so helpless when my mother was sick and dying, but at least Lydia Carter had full control of her faculties right up to the very end. My heart ached for Jaime and his sisters and what they were going through. And with their father gone, they would be orphans at a much younger age than most facing the same situation. At least I still had my dad.

Though lately, it felt like I was losing him, too. I could understand why there was no light in his eyes anymore. If it wasn't for Sophie and Caroline, I was certain the light in my eyes would've been snuffed out as well. But I felt like I was spending most my time fighting for his attention to hold on to the best parts of him. Sometimes, I worried all those good parts died with my mother.

"Come on, Emma, focus," I schooled myself as I tried to reexamine the numbers before my tired eyes. I needed to have a solid understanding of the figures before dinner with Andrew that evening, and I hoped to God he'd be prepared to talk business unlike the other night. Socializing was always a part of the deal, but I wasn't interested in escorting an overgrown frat boy for the duration of this trip. All my father wanted was to secure the merger, but I wanted to make sure we were actually making a sound business decision that wouldn't come back to bite us later.

As I sat working on some figures, I could hear birdsong through the suite window. I smiled to myself when the song struck a chord and grew closer. I jerked my head up and spied a brown-capped rosy finch.

A grin stretched across my face—it was one of my mom's favorites. We would spend hours on the trail, hiking through the beautiful woods behind the resort, and she would point out all the birds, imitating their calls. Later, when Jaime and I became friends, we would sneak out to the same spot, and I would educate him on the birds and plants. I remembered telling him about my mom's favorite bird on one of those hikes.

I swallowed around a lump of emotion at the memory, then looked down, frustrated at the spreadsheet in front of me. It was no wonder I couldn't focus. I had all this beautiful land waiting to be explored, and I was stuck inside staring at numbers.

I scooted back from the desk and dug out my hiking boots and comfy clothes from my suitcase. Before I'd gotten on the plane to Denver, I'd scolded myself for bothering to pack them because I wouldn't have time to enjoy the serenity of woods. It would be work, work, work after all. But now I was grateful for being stubborn enough to keep the clothes in my suitcase.

In minutes, I was dressed and out the door. I left a note for Caroline, reminding her to have the Denver Omelet for breakfast because it was our specialty.

The halls were quiet this time of morning, so I didn't have to interact with too many people as I headed out for my hike. I couldn't help but sneak a peek at the bar as I passed by even though I knew it wouldn't be open for hours. Still, knowing I would see him again soon sent a thrill of excitement through me. Between that and the first gulp of fresh mountain air I inhaled as I stepped outside, I felt high.

I needed to get out more. It was so easy to hide away inside in LA. While there was amazing scenery there, too, the smog and crowds kept me from enjoying the outdoors.

Once I was deep in the woods, though, all the worries I'd been carrying seemed to melt away. I spotted two more songbirds and a golden eagle, and the farther I walked, the more it became a game to see what I could spot. I'd just spied another finch when a strong breeze blew through, rustling the leaves on the trees, and the scent of my mother's perfume overwhelmed me. "Mom?" I breathed, then felt instantly silly.

But when the finch started singing, it didn't seem outside the realm of possibility that it was Mom saying hi. By the time I returned to the resort, I felt dizzy and euphoric from the fresh air.

I marched back to my room with a fresh wave of determination and feeling more at peace than I had in a long time. Suddenly, it didn't seem so crazy that I'd been reunited with Jaime. This place could be magical as long as you respected it and knew when to be still. At least that was what my mother always told me. She'd said one of the hardest things in life to figure out was when it was time to shut your mouth and just be still.

When I opened the door to the suite, Caroline was still in her bathrobe, sitting on the couch eating breakfast and watching *Let's Make a Deal*.

"Oh my God, I've been worried sick about you," she said around a mouthful of Denver Omelet.

I didn't bother to hide my amused smile. "I see that. So worried you could barely eat," I teased.

She swallowed her food hard, then sniffed at me. "We all have our ways of coping. Where have you been?"

"Didn't you read the note? I went for a hike."

"Yeah, but that was like two hours ago."

I raised my eyebrows at her. "So? That's not that long. How long do you think a hike should take?"

She pulled a face. "How the hell should I know? The last time my people hiked was to get the hell out of Ireland. Sullivan thighs haven't hiked shit since the potato famine."

I rolled my eyes. "I'm pretty sure you're full of shit, my dear."

She huffed. "Fine. *These* thighs haven't … well, I take that back. I had to hike to get to those nosebleed seats for that Backstreet Boys concert, but it was totally worth it," she said with a smirk.

I laughed. "Well, I think you would find this 'totally worth it' too. I can't believe I'd forgotten how beautiful it is out there. I can take in a deep breath of fresh air and not start hacking and coughing. It's amazing. Plus, the birds were in fine form singing this morning. I can't wait to do it again tomorrow—you should come with me."

Caroline's eyes widened. "Whoa now, I'm glad you enjoyed your little communion with nature, but let's not get too wild. Besides, I have my eye on some cute little boutiques that are calling my name, so I guess you could consider that my birdsong."

I smiled at her, not surprised by her protestations. "Let me get cleaned up, and we can hit the town. You can get a first-class tour from your own personal Silverpineian ... Silverpineite? Shit, what do we call ourselves?"

"Nuts seems appropriate," Caroline teased. "I'm all for a girls' day out, but I'm surprised. I thought you had to get ready for your business dinner this evening?"

I waved a dismissive hand. "I've bored myself to tears looking at those numbers. Besides, if it means I have to stay a little longer to get the merger done, it's no big deal. You need the time away, and I could use some more time in the mountains."

"Mm-hmm," Caroline said as she set her breakfast plate back onto the room service cart. "And more time with a certain bartender?"

I looked at her sharply but decided not to conceal the smile overtaking my lips. Instead, I shrugged nonchalantly. "We'll see what happens."

Caroline grinned. "That's the Emma I remember. This is going to get interesting."

I certainly hoped so.

Sitting in The Lounge across from Andrew later that evening, I was grateful for my hike that morning and Caroline and I spending the day having fun. She'd been skeptical about how much fun could be had in a place as small as Silverpine, but I easily put her doubts to rest.

It was the first time in a long time I allowed myself to just let loose, and it made me realize how little time I've taken for myself since my mom died.

While I wasn't expecting to have fun at my business dinner with Andrew, I couldn't believe one person could be so boring. We had yet to discuss the merger because he'd been too busy distracting me with stories about his ski trips to Aspen and reunions with his frat brothers, which was more exciting than sleepy little Silverpine. "Not that there's anything wrong with this place," he added quickly, a nervous laugh in his voice. "It's just … so small."

I raised a brow. "Indeed, it is, and that's the way we like it. Despite its size, I have some figures here that show the impact Pine Crest Mountain has on Silverpine and the surrounding communities. Our profit is everyone's profit. And since Get Outdoors has an established brand, I don't think it would be unreasonable to expect a profit within the first year of operation," I said as I pulled out a folder of projections.

I opened the folder, intending to summarize the reports, when Andrew reached out, covering my hand with his own.

I resisted the urge to tug my hand away. "Do we really need to look at those boring old figures? I mean, what are we really talking about here, Emma?"

I couldn't hide the stunned look on my face. I had to deal with a lot of business tactics over the years, but his question was unsettling for reasons I couldn't quite put my finger on. It wouldn't be the first time a business associate tried flirting to get their way, but there was something about his tone that made a chill go up my spine.

I pulled my hand out from beneath his and placed it safely in my lap. "We're talking about creating a boutique version of your family's store and putting it right here in the resort."

"No, no, darlin', think big picture. A scaled-down version of our store is a great first step, but there's so much more we can do here … together," he said expansively, a soft smile curving his lips. He leaned forward across the small table, and at that moment, I wished to God we'd been seated at a less intimate table. He was way too close—close enough for me to smell whiskey on his breath. "Emma, this is the merging of two families. I'm not just talking about business … I'm talking about our families, our legacies. We have an opportunity to make our mark as one. You just have to open your mind and consider possibilities you haven't before."

I scooted back into my chair as far as it would go, uneasy with the turn the conversation was taking. Furrowing my brow, I replied, "Please spell it out for me, Mr. Travers. What possibilities haven't I considered?"

Andrew sat back, deciding his close and personal tactic wasn't having the effect he'd intended. "Well, as I suggested last night, there's a wide expanse of land that has yet to be explored, but you shut me down."

"That's correct, and respectfully, it sounds like I need to do it again because you don't mean explore, do you? You mean expand, develop, tear down, and build, right?"

He laughed nervously. "You make it sound so destructive. I think you're missing out on how exciting something like this could be. We're not taking away from the land—we're making it better."

I held back a laugh. I'd heard that spin on development more times than I cared to count from money hungry investors. How Andrew thought he could make the landscape behind the resort better by demolishing it confounded me.

"While I respect your opinion, I ask you respect mine. The land is nonnegotiable. It belonged to my mother, and she made it very clear when she left it to me that it not be used for profit. She revered this land, and I intend to see that legacy through. There's nothing you can say to change my mind."

For a moment, Andrew studied me with his mouth open like a dead fish before he composed himself and said, "Well, hey, I can respect your convictions. I just think everything doesn't need to be so black and white. That doesn't mean we can't come to a compromise that would make everyone happy. There's still more than enough to work with here."

I looked at him speculatively, unsure of how to move forward. My instinct was to make my stance even more clear, but I could practically hear my father in my ear cautioning me not to ruin the deal with my temper.

It was then the server came to refill our glasses, and I excused myself to the restroom. As soon as I was in the bathroom, I texted Caroline:

Me: Hey, I need an SOS call to get out of this dinner. Call me in five minutes?

I breathed a sigh of relief when she answered almost immediately.

Caroline: On it. Five minutes starting now.

Thank God for Caroline. I smoothed a hand over my hair and made my way back to the table. Andrew was busy chatting away on his phone, glancing at me as I sat back down and mouthing "Sorry."

As he wrapped up his conversation, I pushed the food around on my plate with my fork, not bothering to eat any of it.

"I'm sorry about that. Sometimes all this networking can be downright exhausting. Now, where were we? Ah, yes, we were talking about merging," he said, drawing out the last word, and I smiled tightly, trying to hide my disgust.

I opened my mouth to speak, but before I could get a word out, my phone rang.

Thank you, Caroline.

"Excuse me … You know how it is. I have to take this," I said, slipping my phone from my clutch and stepping into the lobby. "Hello?"

"Hello, Ms. Carter, an emergency requires your attention. Now before you say anything, I need to know … Are you okay getting rid of this guy on your own, or do I need to come down there with a crowbar? Be honest."

I bit back a laugh. "That won't be necessary, but I appreciate the concern."

"Of course. What are friends for? I expect a full report when you get back, though."

"You got it," I promised before I hung up. I glanced up, and my eyes landed on the bar where Jaime was helping a guest. He looked up at that exact moment, and our eyes caught and held. After all this time, he could still make me weak in the knees.

A slow smile stretched across Jaime's lips, and he winked. I smiled back like a teenager with a crush. He turned his attention back to his customer, and I immediately felt the loss of connection.

I walked back to the table, looking apologetic. "Andrew, I am so sorry, but there's an emergency and …"

"And you need to go," he finished.

I nodded, forcing a sheepish expression, and Andrew nodded in understanding. "I get it—I always have a lot of fires to put out. I assume I'll hear from you tomorrow to set up another time to meet?"

"Of course," I promised, already dreading it. Andrew opened his arms for a hug, but I stuck out my hand. He laughed awkwardly and shook my hand before telling me goodnight and slinking out of the restaurant.

I hovered near the table until I was sure Andrew was out of sight, then escaped into the bar, relief pouring over me at the idea of being in Jaime's presence.

I headed straight toward Jaime, who was grinning at me.

"What happened to your fancy business dinner?" he asked as I slipped my butt onto a stool.

I shrugged. "It was a bust, which is why I could use a Gin Fizz right about now."

"Coming up," he replied as he grabbed a shaker. "I would feel bad your dinner didn't go well, but selfishly, I'm glad because you're here earlier than I expected."

I felt myself blush. "Well, those dinners are boring, and I'd rather spend my time talking to someone interesting."

His eyebrows shot up. "And you think I'm interesting?"

I huffed out a laugh. "So modest. You *know* you're usually the most interesting man in the room."

He barked a laugh. "Isn't that the guy in the Dos Equis commercial?"

"I'm just saying you could give him a run for his money."

Jaime leaned closer—close enough I could smell his cologne. He smelled like cedar with a hint of bergamot and something uniquely Jaime.

That was when my stomach growled. Loud. I felt my face heat with embarrassment.

"Was that …" he started.

I nodded. "Yes … and that was totally embarrassing," I lamented.

"Did you not eat at that fancy dinner tonight?" he asked with a raised eyebrow.

I shook my head. "Kind of lost my appetite having to deal with that blowhard …" I began before stopping myself as Jaime listened with amusement. "I mean, having to deal with that promising investor," I amended, slapping an exaggerated smile on my face.

He chuckled. "Well, I'll tell you what. Why don't you work on getting a little less gin and a little more water into your system, and I'll go make you something to eat."

I shook my head. "Oh no, Jaime, I couldn't ask you to do that."

"You didn't, I'm offering," he said with a grin before something caught his eye over my shoulder. I turned to find Caroline with a feline smile on her lips as she glanced between the two of us.

"Well, hello there," she practically sang as she slipped onto the stool beside me, reaching her hand out to Jaime. "I'm Caroline, Emma's best friend. You must be Jaime."

Jaime shook her hand, his grin widening. "Hello, Caroline, it's nice to meet you. I was just going to rustle up something to eat for my starving soldier here. You wouldn't happen to be hungry, would you?"

Caroline's eyes lit with amusement as she rested her chin on a fist. "Oh Jaime, that's my eternal state of being."

Jaime laughed, and the rich sound sent shivers down my spine. "Okay—two Jaime specials coming up," he said, throwing a towel over his shoulder. "You two sit tight, and I'll be back before you know it."

As soon as he was out of sight, Caroline looked at me in wonder. "Oh. My. God," she marveled. "He's cooking for you already. I see why you've been pining after him for so long."

"Caroline," I hissed. "Keep your voice down. You have the subtly of a freight train."

She made a face. "Uh, I hate to break it to you, Emma, but there's nothing subtle about this whole situation. I mean, when I walked in here, that man looked like he was two seconds away from devouring you."

A happy warmth spread through me at her observation, but I didn't say anything.

"Besides, you had to know I was going to come check on you after that SOS call. I'm assuming your associate had to have been behaving like a total creep to make you call me."

I sighed. "Well, maybe not a total creep, but he was fast approaching," I paused, turning to face Caroline. "It's weird. Before I would have breezed through that dinner no matter how uncomfortable I was in order to get the deal done. But there's something about being here … I don't know. I just didn't have it in me to put up with it tonight."

Caroline nodded sympathetically. "Maybe Mama Carter's spirit is reminding you it's not your job to take everybody's shit."

I laughed. "I can't imagine my mother putting it like that, but maybe you're right … and based on our recent experiences, it would seem we both need to embrace that sentiment."

Caroline grimaced. "Amen to that."

It was then that Jaime returned with a tray in his arms. "Ladies, dinner is served," he said, presenting us with two plates that each held a burger with all the fixings, a side of fries, and little cups filled with ketchup.

My eyes widened as the smell hit my nostrils and my empty stomach. "Is that …" I started.

"Oh, it is, Mabel's secret recipe," Jaime announced with relish. "It's been a long time, but I know that recipe like the back of my hand. I only wish I could get my hands on a couple of chocolate milkshakes, and then you could have the full experience."

I couldn't stop the grin that took over my mouth. "I can't believe you went to all this trouble."

Jaime shook his head. "Anything for you, Bella," he said in a low voice, and prickles of pleasure raced down my spine at the mention of the nickname he'd given me when we were younger. I still remember the first time he'd called me that, explaining it meant beautiful.

Our eyes held for a long moment before Caroline's moan interrupted. "Wow, you were not lying about this burger, Emma," she mumbled around a mouthful of burger.

"Well, tell me if it still holds up," Jaime said, gesturing toward my plate.

I picked up the hefty burger, my mouth watering from the smell, and when I took that first bite, a flood of memories assaulted my senses from the taste.

My eyes shut in rapture. It tasted heavenly, but knowing Jaime's hands created it made it all the better.

I opened my eyes and met Jaime's gaze as he watched me hungrily. I swallowed hard around the bite of food as a different appetite was awakened.

Caroline cleared her throat loudly. "You know, as fun as this has been and as much as I would like to get to know the legendary Jaime, I think it might be better to take this in a doggy bag."

I looked sharply at Caroline, feeling the need to tell her, "You don't need to do that."

She winked at me before saying, "I assure you, no one needs to witness me consuming this burger—it's about to get wild. So if you'll excuse me, I think my burger and I need to be alone."

Jaime had already pulled out a cardboard box and was helping Caroline pack up her food along with a complimentary cocktail for the road.

"Well, Jaime, it was lovely meeting you, and I hope we can talk more later, but right now, I have a date with this burger," Caroline declared.

"Totally understand. It was nice to meet a friend of Emma's."

Caroline beamed at Jaime—my normally suspicious friend had been charmed. She rose from her stool and hugged me. "I'll catch up with you later."

"Enjoy that burger," Jaime said, his sexy smile further crumbling my resolve. God, that smile used to make me feel all the things, and it had only magnified in power in the years we'd been apart.

It was then Joey rushed to the bar. "Jaime, I'm sorry to interrupt, but we have a situation with a guest."

Jaime shot us both an apologetic look. "I'll be right back," he said before stepping around the bar and following Joey.

Caroline looked at me, eyebrows drawn up. "Emma," she exclaimed, "I thought you were being a little dramatic all these years, but girl, you definitely undersold him. And for the record, that man has plans for you."

I shook my head. "Would you calm down? We're old friends catching up on lost time. That's all," I said, unsure who I was trying to convince, Caroline or myself.

She huffed out a laugh. "You can tell yourself that all you want, but from my vantage point, you are two seconds away from doing it on this bar." She stopped cold, and a wicked grin stole over her mouth. "Now wouldn't that be a picture for old Daddy Moneybags?" she asked, using the nickname she'd given my father, a man she wasn't particularly fond of given how he'd been acting lately. "And as a token of my love and admiration," she continued, "I'm delaying the consumption of this burger to stop by the front desk and get my own room."

I felt a weird combination of panic and excitement threading through me at her suggestion. "Caroline, that's really not necessary. I seriously doubt …"

She put up a hand to stop me. "Save your breath, Emma. All I'm asking is for you to keep an open mind, and this way, you can't use me crashing in your suite as an excuse. I refuse to be a cockblock."

I opened my mouth to protest, but Caroline just grinned, snatching up her to-go cocktail and box and giving me a wink before floating out of the bar and into the lobby.

Despite the confusion her "analysis" was creating for me, I was grateful she was here. Being back here without my mom and reuniting with Jaime brought up so many feelings. I didn't think I could manage it without my best friend's counsel.

I just wish she hadn't pointed out Jaime looked like he wanted to devour me. I shivered at the thought. That Jaime might want me in that way made me feel dizzy with anticipation.

As if my thoughts had summoned him back, Jaime reappeared behind the bar. "Sorry about that," he said, slightly breathless.

"They must have had you running. I hope everything's okay."

His smile widened, and he leaned on his elbows, his mouth inches from mine. "I'm not out of breath from running back over here."

"You're not?" I squeaked.

"Nope. It's because when I rounded the corner, I saw Emma Carter sitting on one of my barstools."

I felt my cheeks flush. "Jaime Acosta, are you flirting with me?" I teased although I knew better. Jaime had never been a flirt, just unfailingly honest and a little intense with no filter. He wasn't afraid to say what was on his mind or ask for what he wanted. It was something I'd always admired about him. I spent my life biting my tongue and verbally dancing my way around social interactions and uncomfortable situations.

Jaime's eyes drifted to my mouth again, and I had to work to suppress the shiver dancing down my spine. "Emma, you know that's not my style," he said in a low voice.

"I know," I whispered.

He tilted his head, looking at me curiously. "You know, I've been going on and on telling you all about what I've been up to, but you have yet to tell me what's been happening with you."

I don't know why his words made me feel like there was a rock on my chest. Maybe I didn't want to admit to him I'd spent most of the last twelve years doing my father's bidding. So, I sucked in a deep breath and stuck to safer topics. "Well, um, I went to Stanford."

"I heard about that. I was surprised you went that far away," he said idly as polished glasses.

There was that heaviness again, but the truth was, I hadn't expected to go to California either. I wanted to stay close to my mom and Jaime, but after he and I … well, after everything went down, I needed to get away to some place that didn't remind me of everything I'd left behind. So I traded in the snowy mountains of Colorado for the beaches of California and hoped the change would be enough to distract me. I'd been wrong, but I'd built my life out there anyway.

I cleared my throat. "Yeah, it's not where I expected to wind up, but life's funny that way," I said. His eyes caught on mine, and all the old hurt came rushing back, socking me in the chest. I'd been walking around in agony all of this time thinking I was alone. And yet, based on the look in Jaime's eyes, I hadn't been the only one feeling that way. Had he been hanging on all this time the way I had?

Needing a break from the intensity of the moment, I huffed out a nervous laugh. "I, um, rowed for Stanford, too. We won a few championships—not to toot my own horn."

His expression relaxed into an easy smile. "Toot away, that's awesome. You were always a talented athlete. I'm glad to hear you kept it up."

"I'm hoping to get out to Rainbow Lake before I leave."

"Have you determined how long do we get to keep you?" he asked.

I swallowed hard at his question because there was something in his tone that had me thinking about the soon-to-be-empty suite upstairs.

"At least a week? This negotiation will be a little trickier than I first thought."

"Well, I wish I could say I'm sorry it isn't going more smoothly, but selfishly, I'm happy to hear it," he said, leaning closer. Suddenly, the bar felt impossibly small, and despite the voice of reason in my head screaming to create some space, I couldn't look away from Jaime and those soulful brown eyes. They still seemed to see right through me.

There's no hiding from this man—there never was. I hadn't been able to hide from him twelve years ago, so why did I think I'd be able to resist him now?

Jaime

O ld habits died hard, and evidently, there wasn't anything in the world that could quell my desire for Emma Carter.

I didn't press her for information about her life after college—about what it was like to give her life over to her old man, because if I had to guess, it hadn't been all sunshine and roses. I suspect Mr. Carter ruled with an iron fist, and without Mrs. Carter there to keep him in line, he probably imagined himself unstoppable.

Judging by the weariness in Emma's eyes, I would guess her father's moral boundaries had gone up in smoke with his late wife. That and the intense relief that overcame Emma when she walked in here after her "business dinner date."

After all these years, I still felt this possessive urge to keep her as close to me as possible and protect her from anyone who made her feel weary.

The spark in Emma's eyes when we were kids was barely there now, and while most people would agree adulthood had a way of dulling such things, this was different. My instinct told me she'd been put in an impossible position.

Or maybe that was just wishful thinking. I long entertained the notion there was more to Emma's decision than loyalty to her family when she cut me out of her life years ago.

Come on, Jaime. You need to stop living in the past.

But it was difficult to do that when she was looking at me with so much need in her eyes. I noticed the way her face flushed when I got close—and that she didn't pull away. My eyes drifted to her full lips, wondering if she still tasted the same—felt the same.

I was about to find out when Joey called out, "Hey, boss, we're all done here. Did you want to check it out before we go?"

I didn't move a muscle, but Emma's eyes widened, and she adjusted herself, regrettably pulling back.

I bit back an irritated groan, wanting to throttle Joey for interrupting us even though he was just doing his job. I was the one behaving inappropriately, mere seconds away from kissing Emma out in the open for everyone to see.

I cleared my throat before calling out without breaking eye contact with Emma, "I'm sure it's fine. Go ahead and clock out."

The corners of her mouth quirked up, and she said, "I don't want to get in your way."

"You're never in the way. Besides, I hire good people. If they say it's clean, then it is. I just need to shut down our POS system, and then I'll walk you to your room."

There was the eternal politeness I found both charming and exasperating. "You really don't have to."

This time, I did groan in frustration. "I know, Emma, but I want to. I'm not done with you yet," I said before I could think better of it even though no truer words had been spoken. We had unfinished business, and I wouldn't let this opportunity slip through my fingers. "Besides," I continued, "You never know who's lurking in the mean halls of Pine Crest Mountain Resort," I teased.

"Okay," she breathed. "If you insist, you may escort me to my room," she relented, but I could hear the laughter in her voice.

I closed out the books and shut down the computers like a man whose ass was on fire and then rushed around the bar holding out my elbow like I was a country squire about to escort the lady of the manor to her palatial space, which ironically, I was.

If anyone would have told me the simple touch of someone's arm could be erotic, I would have thought they were nuts, and yet it felt like an electric current surging between us where our arms met.

"Do you remember touring the expansion of this place with me after all the drywall was up?" she asked as we shared a thankfully empty elevator.

I laughed, my heart racing even harder, realizing she was bringing up the memory of our first kiss.

"How could I forget? That's when you lured me into a corner and took advantage of me," I teased.

She swatted at my arm, biting her lip but smiling. The elevator came to a stop, and we stepped out onto the floor, looking at one another, our arms still intertwined at the elbow. "Oh, um, my room is at the end of the hall."

We began the long walk, and I was grateful her room was on the opposite end of the expansive hallway, so I could delay the inevitable moment when we'd say good-night.

"I remember you coming over to the new construction site I was working on with my dad since we'd finished framing the addition to the resort," I said.

My dad's team had built the bones of the structure, and then another team hung and finished the drywall while my dad's crew moved on to the next job—a gas station on Route 14.

I'd loved working with my dad and making some extra money, but once the job was done, I didn't have an excuse to see my beautiful new friend Emma. My Dad had teased me about not enjoying the scenery at the new job site—a dozen sweaty construction workers. He'd sighed and clapped me on the back. "I know we're not nearly as nice to look at as that redhead, but you'll see her again," he'd encouraged.

It'd felt like I'd never be lucky enough to see her again until later that afternoon when a familiar BMW pulled up to the construction site.

I remembered how my heart had thudded in my chest as I waited with bated breath to see who would emerge from that car. I couldn't for the life of me fathom why Mrs. Carter would have come all the out there, but then that familiar redhead emerged from the car, and the next thing I knew, a very determined Emma marched over to me, her ponytail bobbing from side to side with every step.

She'd beamed when our eyes met. "Jaime!" she'd said with excitement. "I have great news. They finished the drywall at the resort." I'd supposed that was great news for her family, but I wasn't sure why I should be excited about it until she was standing right in front of me—her sweet scent wafting around me and threatening to make my brain short circuit. "I thought if you could take a break, maybe I could give you a tour, you know, show you how all your hard work is shaping up," she'd said with bright, hopeful eyes.

I hadn't been able to hold back my smile, but it had quickly melted when I realized it would be at least a few more hours before I could take a break. But that was when my dad had called out, "Jaime! We've got it covered here—take the rest of the day."

My father was never one for knocking off early. He'd believed every hour of pay was one more hour of security for our family. I had been about to question him, but he'd thrown me a stern look, so I kept my mouth shut. Emma had watched our exchange with hope in her eyes, and when I turned to her and said, "That sounds great. Maybe I can take you to Mabel's for a burger afterward?" her smile had tugged at my heart and made desire streak through me.

"That would be nice," she'd replied as I packed up my tools. My dad had waved at us as we walked to the BMW, and it warmed me from the inside out as Emma waved back and said, "Thanks for letting me have him for a bit, Mr. Acosta."

I'd seen the amused smile on my dad's face, and Emma's words had caused a fresh stirring in me that was hard to control as a young man. But my arousal came to a screeching halt as we approached Mrs. Carter's expensive car. I'd been on the site for hours. I was sweaty and dirty, so I hesitated.

Ever watchful, Emma had said, "I'm sorry about the mess in the car. A couple of friends and I went hiking this morning and tracked in a bunch of mud."

"Your mom won't be upset?" I'd questioned, sensing Emma was trying to comfort me before the fact.

She shook her head. "My mom? She's the one who hikes in the most dirt," she'd laughed, and I'd felt instantly at ease, even with my grimy jeans sitting in the passenger seat of Emma's mother's car. From there, she'd taken me to the newly dry walled site, and as we'd walked through the empty halls, she'd slipped her hand into mine and went on and on about the plans for the expansion and everything that needed to happen before they unveiled it. Finally, I couldn't take it anymore. As soon as we'd reached an abandoned corner, I'd stopped her nervous chattering by leaning down and laying my lips across hers.

I thought about that day often, the first brush of her lips that had me hooked. And to this day, I haven't been able to unhook myself—I've never wanted to.

"Excuse me," she laughed. "You're rewriting history, Mr. Acosta, because I distinctly remember you cutting me off mid-sentence to kiss me."

We were approaching the double doors at the end of the hall that led to the Carter family suite, and a knot of dread began forming in my gut. Our moment was almost over. "Well, you can hardly blame me. I'd been wanting to kiss you all summer, and we were finally alone," I asserted as we stopped in front of her door.

She turned to face me then, a little more of that spark in her eyes now.

I looked down at her, reveling in the way she tilted her head upward, staring into my eyes, and the loneliness I saw in hers tore at me. Not just because I couldn't stand the thought of her being lonely, but because it was the very thing that had been plaguing me for years. I'd had relationships, but none of them were Emma, and she was who I wanted. "I had no choice but to kiss you before I lost my nerve."

She huffed out a laugh. "I've never known you to be short on nerve, Jaime," she breathed.

"It's rare, that's for sure. But if I'm being honest, I could use a little extra nerve today, too."

Something lit in her eyes, and a familiar heat rushed through me as she murmured, "Then let me give you some of mine." Then she rose on her toes, and like a magnet, our mouths had no choice but to meet. At the first taste of her, I had to bite back a groan and curl my hands into fists at my sides to keep from grabbing her and manhandling her like a caveman.

But Emma had other plans because she curled her hands into my shirt, yanking me down so I had no choice but to slant my mouth to kiss her more deeply. The action made her lose her balance, and because of her hold on me, we both stumbled back until we bumped against the wall.

We broke apart, laughing, but when our eyes met, all laughter stopped. Her eyes were glassy with need, and my mouth went for hers with a vengeance. I needed to taste her again like I needed air.

When my tongue touched hers, there was no going back. I speared my fingers into her hair, the silky tresses twining around my fingers, and a hungry moan echoed through the air. It took me a moment to realize it had come from Emma's throat and not my own.

This wasn't like any of the stolen kisses from our youth, not with the way her hands were rubbing against my chest. And God, the taste of her … I felt like I was home after being away for too damn long.

I didn't know how I would stop when Emma abruptly shoved me away and looked up at me with wild, worried eyes, then breathed, "We have to stop."

Emma

I didn't know what possessed me, but once we were alone, Jaime overwhelmed me. His scent, his warmth and charm. Everything I'd missed about him compelled me to act. It was as if I didn't have control of my body.

My lack of control scared me even as the taste of Jaime thrilled me. What would happen if we took it further? Could my heart handle it when it inevitably ended?

My brain was fighting with my body, which was screaming for more of Jaime's touches. It frightened me how much I wanted him, which was why I pushed him away so forcefully.

But then something strange happened. It was as if the cosmic presence of both Sophie and Caroline converged, and I could practically hear their voices screaming at me to "let go." Ever since my mom died, I'd been holding onto every little thing as if my life depended on it because I was terrified of what else I might lose.

But the truth was I'd already lost Jaime, so I really had nothing to lose. Why not have some fun? Why not get answers to some long burning questions about Jaime? Like what it would be like to spend all night in his arms—or what it would feel like to have him inside me. That question had driven me to near madness a few times in my adult life.

When I shoved him away, though, the wounded look in his eyes told me everything I needed to know. Despite what I'd said, I didn't want to stop. I wanted the heat back in his eyes and his hands on me, so moments after I pushed him away, I told the sexy man in front of me, "What the hell am I saying? I don't want to stop." Then I grabbed his shirt again, yanking him to me, and our mouths crashed together.

He groaned against my lips, and my hands ran over his taut chest and stomach. I had vivid memories of what he looked like without a shirt on when we would go swimming as kids. But I suspected those broad shoulders and muscular arms I'd been admiring since I got back matched that of a mature man, one who would make me forget, if only momentarily, all the pain and loss.

His mouth traveled over my cheek and down my neck, and the feel of his lips against my skin warmed me from the inside out. "Jaime," I breathed. "Come inside with me."

His eyes were dark and wild as they looked into mine. "Are you sure, Bella?"

I nodded enthusiastically. "Yes, I'm sure." I wouldn't let any niggling worries ruin this moment—I wanted him, and I wasn't about to let him go.

His eyes dipped to my mouth and then down the rest of my body as I rushed to grab my clutch, my hands shaking with excitement as I dug for my room key. It was only the size of a wallet, yet I was fumbling to find the key when Jaime reached his hands out, covering my shaking hands with his large, steadying ones.

"Let me help," he said in his deep, reassuring voice. Keeping one hand on mine, his other reached inside my clutch and effortlessly snagged the key card. I was grateful for his steadiness because I felt like I would come apart if I didn't get in his arms soon.

He flashed the key card on the sensor, and the door clicked open. Then he held it up between two fingers, offering it back to me as he grabbed the door handle.

It wasn't lost on me that the next time I walked out of this room, I would finally know what it was like to be with Jaime, to share myself completely with him.

With a shaky breath, I follow him in and shut the door behind us with a definitive click. Jaime looked at me for a long moment in the dim light from the lamp Caroline must have left on.

I dared a glance around the room to see Caroline had indeed cleared out all her things. Then I returned my nervous gaze back to him. "Jaime?" I started, unsure of what to say next, but he seemed to understand my hesitancy because he answered by reaching out and grabbing my hand, gently tugging me to him until I fell into his arms. His other hand stroked my cheek.

"This is like a dream," he admitted, his breath fanning over my lips as he stared down into my eyes, and I let myself get lost in his big brown soulful eyes just like I used to. They felt like home.

"I've imagined it a million times," I said before I could bite my tongue. Embarrassment burned my cheeks at the admission, but his sexy smile only grew.

"You have?" he asked in wonder, continuing to stroke his fingers over my cheek, somehow soothing a part of me I didn't know could be calmed by mere physical touch.

Feeling a little less embarrassed by his response, I nodded. "I guess that's surprising considering …" I trailed off, not wanting to bring up how I'd ended things.

"No, it's not surprising," he said, his voice rolling over me in a sensuous yet comforting way. "You and I have unfinished business, Emma," he said before leaning down and capturing my mouth again, this time more slowly like he had all the time in the world. I reveled in the taste of him and how strong and reassuring his arms felt banded around me.

As much as I enjoyed the comfort of his arms, my body wanted more, and I decided that, at least for tonight, my body would call the shots. So, with a quaking breath, I reached up and gently pushed off Jaime's shoulders, breaking our kiss. He looked dismayed for a split second before his eyes followed my fingers as they methodically unbuttoned his shirt.

He watched me intently with his dark gaze, the heat in his eyes emboldening me as I shoved his shirt off his shoulders.

Once he was bare chested, I let my eyes take in the sculpted muscles, the light sprinkling of hair on his chest and how it trailed down his defined abs and below his belt. Giddiness raced through me as I trailed my fingertips down his chest and over his stomach, relishing in the way his stomach muscles tightened at my touch. He watched me as I leaned forward and touched my lips to his chest, slowly trailing kisses over his hot skin, darting my tongue out for a taste now and then as I slowly sank to my knees before him.

I hadn't realized he was holding his breath until my fingers started working at undoing his belt and his breath came out in a hiss and then his fingers were in my hair, gently pulling my head back to look up at him.

How many times had I fantasized about being in this very position, looking up at the man I could never seem to forget?

"Emma," he growled. "You have no idea how many times I've thought of you in this position," he admitted. "But I'm not sure I could survive that right now. I need to be inside you, to feel you wrapped around me," he said in anguish.

Feeling even more emboldened, I rose to my feet, not breaking eye contact as I stood, my fingers still working at his belt and then the snap and zipper of his pants. "Then that's where you shall be," I said as I shoved his pants down over his boxers.

The corner of his mouth quirked upward, and he lunged forward, cupping my face in his hands. "I swear, Bella, you're going to be the death of me … but I can't think of a better way to go," he whispered before he took my mouth again. This time, his lips and tongue were much more insistent, taking possession of me even as he shimmied out of his pants.

My hands went to the elastic waistband of his boxers, and I shoved those down, too, Jaime releasing me long enough to kick them to the side. When he reached for me again, however, I stopped him by placing a palm on his chest while my other hand went to explore the hard, impressive length before me.

I wrapped my fingers around his girth and smiled at the way he sucked in a sharp breath. I gave it a few tentative strokes, enjoying how hard he was for me. "Of all the fantasies I've had," I said, stroking him a little more firmly now, "this is better than I imagined," I told him in a low voice.

He huffed out a strangled laugh as he watched me intensely beneath those midnight lashes. "I aim to please," he teased.

I smiled at him then, "Thank God for that," I said, still stroking him as I leaned into him for another soul-searing kiss.

After a long moment, he broke the kiss abruptly, panting as he looked down into my face. "Bella," he breathed raggedly, eyeing me darkly. "You have way too many clothes on."

I smiled at him coyly as I released him and stepped back. I watched his expression as I reached behind me and unzipped the back of my dress, the thin straps slipping from my shoulders beneath the weight of the shimmery material. I let the dress fall on its own to the floor, puddling around my matching heels.

A growl ripped from his throat, and he stepped forward, snaking his arm around my waist, then bending down to slip his other arm behind my knees to lift me into his arms.

He held me to him effortlessly as if I weighed nothing and let his hungry eyes rove down my body before swinging his gaze back to mine. "As soon as we hit the sheets, that scrap of fabric you call panties is coming off," he warned before glancing toward my feet and turning back to me. "But the heels stay on."

Jaime set me down on the bed, and the sensation of the silky sheets at my back and Jaime's hard body sliding in between my legs as he lowered himself over me was mind altering.

His mouth attacked mine, and then it was trailing fervent kisses and nibbles, licking at the sensitive skin of my neck, shoulders, and chest.

His hands skated up my waist, cupping the heavy weight of my breasts, and it felt like his mouth was determined to taste every square inch of the two orbs. When his hot mouth finally closed over one of my painfully hard nipples, I cried out, digging my fingers into his thick hair, my hips involuntarily bucking upward against his erection.

If I thought the sensation of his mouth sucking at my nipple was mind blowing, it was nothing compared to the friction between his hard cock and my still covered pussy. I could feel how wet I was against the silky material of my panties, and my grinding made it even worse.

Jaime growled against my skin, his mouth moving more frantically now down my stomach, and I missed the heat of his erection against my center. But when he shoved his shoulders in between my shaking thighs, I knew I was about to receive the contact I so desperately needed.

He was not gentle with the scrap of fabric still covering me, tearing them away easily, and I'd never been so delighted to see something so completely ruined.

Jaime groaned at the sight of me, and his gaze met mine briefly before he focused completely on what was right in front of him. I suppressed a shiver at the way he licked his lips before placing tender kisses over my quivering opening. "Jaime," I breathed, my hands fisting the sheets next to my hips, preparing for what was to come.

His breath was hot over my exposed skin as his fingers gently explored my slick folds, and my moans filled the air as his fingers grew more confident in their caresses. When the pad of his thumb rubbed my clit, I nearly bolted from the bed, the sensation so intense I cried out his name.

My reaction seemed to spur him on because before I could completely come back down to earth, he slipped a finger inside and started stroking, slowly at first, before adding a second one.

I fought for breath as Jaime masterfully worked my pussy, stroking in and out until suddenly his hot mouth attached itself to my clit and relentlessly sucked on me. I was overwhelmed with sensations—and the knowledge that it was Jaime in between my thighs pushed me even closer to the edge.

His fingers continued to work in tandem with his mouth, ratcheting up the pressure in my core as his other hand reached up and teased a swollen nipple.

"Fuck, Jaime. I'm going to come," I cried out.

My orgasm crashed through me, and I was grateful my room was at the end of a long hallway; otherwise, I was certain the entire floor would have heard my cries of pleasure.

I'd never come so hard in my life, and as my heart struggled to calm down, I wondered if I would ever recover from being with Jaime. He rose from between my legs with a satisfied grin on his face. "That was fucking amazing. You're amazing."

He crawled up the bed and settled on top of me, kissing me slowly and thoroughly. Everything about him was intoxicating—his scent, his taste, his breath. I was completely lost in him, anticipating the moment when he'd thrust into me for the first time when panic struck.

I abruptly pushed him away and said, "Jaime, I just realized—I don't have protection."

"No? Then what are those?" he asked, nodding to the bedside table.

I followed his gaze, and to my surprise, there were a half dozen condoms strewn over the tabletop. *Caroline.*

I winced as I turned back to him. "Uh, those aren't mine," I began, my cheeks flush with embarrassment. "Caroline was staying with me and must have left them."

Jaime grinned widely. "Well, thank you, Caroline."

I laughed, shaking my head as I debated whether I would hug or scold Caroline later. Then I reached over and snatched a condom off the table, handing it to him. "Weren't you saying something about needing to feel me wrapped around you?"

His playful expression turned dark. "Bella, I've waited an eternity."

He leaned back on one elbow and quickly rolled on the condom, then positioned himself in between my legs. I reached for him and whispered, "Jaime, I need to feel you inside me, please."

Something feral flashed in his eyes as he positioned himself at my entrance. The erotic image of watching him nudge inside me was almost as intense as feeling him stretch me wide as he invaded.

A long sigh escaped my mouth when he fully seated himself inside me, and I dug my fingers into his muscular shoulders as he began to move. "Bella," he groaned, "your pussy feels even better than I imagined ... so hot and tight." I could sense he was trying to take it slow, but my body didn't want him to go slow.

I kissed him feverishly, moaning into his mouth before pulling away. "Jaime," I whispered with urgency. "Please.

Don't hold back. I *need* you to give it to me—everything you've got."

His already molten eyes burned hotter at my words, and he responded by kissing me thoroughly before one of his hands slid to my hip, clutching it like it was a lifeline. He picked up the pace, driving into me with a force that had my head spinning and cries of pleasure ripping from my throat.

"Christ, Emma. You feel so fucking good," he growled as he thrust in and out of me, his mouth hovering over mine. Feeling our breaths fuse together along with our bodies was enough to set me off, tightening and spasming around his hardness.

"Jaime," I breathed. "I'm going to come again," I almost whined. I wanted it to last, but I could only take so much, and I'd never felt this good before.

"That's it, Emma. Come for me again, squeeze my cock with that gorgeous pussy. I want to feel you tight around me," he managed in between breaths.

He leaned down to capture my mouth with his own, and when his tongue dueled with mine, imitating the moves his hips were making, I lost it. My orgasm crashed over me, and I cried into his mouth while he happily drank in the sound, his hips going even faster, chasing his own orgasm. "Fuck," he bit off as he came hard inside me.

He collapsed on top of me, and we held each other, a sweaty tangle of limbs, just listening to one another's breathing as we slowly calmed down. I loved feeling the weight of him on me and tried to not let my mind wander and think about what might happen next or what I should say. I just wanted to stay in this moment and enjoy every second as I ran my fingers through Jaime's thick, silky hair.

I almost thought he'd fallen asleep by the sound of his deep, even breathing until he raised his head and looked at me with sleepy, sated eyes.

"We have a problem here, Emma," he said in his sexy, rumbly voice. His words had my heart racing in dread.

I swallowed around the lump in my throat. Was this the part where he told me this was a one-time thing, and we couldn't let it happen again? "What's that?" I managed to get out even though I would have loved nothing more than to stall.

"Well, I know you have this big merger you're work-ing on, and I have a full-time job, but we're going to need to find some extra hours in the day to make up for lost time," he said with a smile. "Now that I know how amazing you taste and feel wrapped around me—not to mention how hot you sound when you come—I'm going to need a lot more of my sweet Emma." He leaned down then and gave me a slow, bone-melting, sensual kiss, and I sighed with relief into his mouth.

When we finally pulled apart, I smiled up at him. "Well, that could be a challenge, but I think we're up to the task. And speaking of tasks, we still have some unfinished business, Jaime," I said, my eyes exploring his nude body suggestively.

He chuckled at my perusal and kissed me again, pushing me back down on the pillows. "Then we better get to work."

Jaime

nfinished business …

U That seemed to be a theme with Emma and me. Only now I knew with startling clarity my long-held suspicions were true. I didn't have "unfinished business" with Emma. *I would never be finished with her.*

It was something I'd wondered often over the years. In my moments of practicality, I would tell myself the reason the memory of her hung on so forcefully was because we'd had no closure. After our massive fight following my run-in with her father, she'd made it known she wouldn't choose me over her family, and then she was gone. I'd thought she was gone forever.

Then in my more morose moments of missing her, I thought that maybe if I could just get her out of my system, I could finally find some peace.

But now that I'd spent the night with her, woken up with her in my arms, it was clear there would be no getting her out of my system despite how she felt about our time together.

I had no idea how the rest of the week would unfold or what conclusion she may come to regarding us. She seemed to be the same Emma I'd known long ago, but I knew deep down that couldn't be the whole truth. Too much life had happened to both of us in the last twelve years. Emma Carter, with the bouncy red ponytail, had spent the last several years in expensive business suits having even more expensive dinners with clients and negotiating deals worth more than I would make in my lifetime.

She was not the same innocent young woman who'd raced out of Colorado, leaving my broken heart behind. I'd be foolish to assume giving her multiple orgasms and whispering sweet words would be enough to make her stay.

As my mind pondered that thought, I knew I was in serious trouble. I wanted her to stay. I already knew I needed her like I needed my next breath. The question was, did she feel the same way?

I walked out of her room after another early morning romp, determined to enjoy the moment and not over-think the situation. I couldn't predict what Emma's next move would be, but she'd always been more pragmatic than me. That had been our dynamic since the beginning—I was driven by passion and instinct, and she was ruled by reason and predictability.

Thankfully, she promised to see me again that night. I didn't think anything could sour my good mood that day as I drove home … until I walked through the door, and a teacup whizzed past my head and shattered against the wall.

"You have a lot of nerve showing up here after being out catting around all night, Stefan," my mother screamed from her perch on a stool in the kitchen. She looked me up and down with disdain in her eyes. "Don't you dare come near me. I don't want to smell some cheap hussy's perfume on you!"

Maria rushed in from the living room, her face stricken by the commotion. She looked at me apologetically before rushing over to our mother. I knew better than to defend myself.

"Mama," Maria said softly to our mother, "This isn't Papa. It's Jaime, your son," she explained gently.

My mom looked at me as if she'd never seen me before, then whispered, "Jaime?"

"Yes, Mama," I answered softly.

Her lips pressed together in a line of consternation. "Of course, I knew it was you," she said, throwing up a frustrated hand. "Now come help me get my big pan out so I can start you some breakfast."

"Oh, Mama, you really don't have to …" I started, but Maria shook her head in warning behind our mother. I rushed into the small kitchen and squatted down to retrieve the heavy frying pan my mother used to cook nearly everything.

When I set the pan down on the stove for her, my mother looked up at me with a doting smile and cupped my cheek lovingly, just as she had when I was a boy, the action making my throat clog with emotion. I didn't know how many more moments like this I would get.

"Why don't you go clean up, mijo. Breakfast will be ready by the time you're done," she said, pinching my cheek lightly before turning to the stove, effectively dismissing me.

Maria gave me a look of gratitude for playing along as I backed out of the kitchen, following my mother's orders and heading for the shower to clean up. The last thing I wanted was to wash off Emma's scent, but I also knew she was now imprinted on me in a way that could never be washed away.

As I headed down the hall, I lamented what was now becoming a familiar situation with my mom. This wasn't the first time she'd mistaken me for my father. Considering my resemblance to the man, it wasn't surprising. What was disconcerting was that every time she mistook me for my father, she was accusing him of having a wandering eye.

Stefan Acosta was the most faithful man I'd ever known. But Mama had a jealous streak that only worsened once we'd immigrated to the United States. She was convinced the wealthy women of Silverpine would take one look at the tall, dark, and charming Stefan and fall over themselves for a taste of something "exotic."

And it was true, my father had attracted his fair share of female attention. The man had a charming smile and was easy to talk to—but he'd only had eyes for Mama.

For her part, Mama had often told me I'd gotten my dad's smile, and I needed to be careful with who I flashed it at.

I dreaded how she'd react if she found out I was seeing Emma again. She'd always liked Emma as a person—declaring her to be a "sweet girl." But she'd warned me back then not to get too attached because that "family of hers" would not be so welcoming. I'd brushed off her concerns. I'd already met Mrs. Carter several times, and she'd seemed to like me. But I found out the hard way it wouldn't be Mrs. Carter who would be the problem.

Once I was in the shower and the scent of Emma wafted in the steamy air, I couldn't think of anything other than her. Nor could I stop the goofy smile from overtaking my mouth.

Mere hours before, I'd held the woman of my dreams in my arms, and while it felt surreal, it also felt … right. More than I wanted to entertain at that moment.

After my shower, I headed back downstairs, the smell of breakfast wafting to my nose.

Mornings where Mama felt good enough to cook were rare, so I would enjoy the moment, but as I rounded the corner, I saw her "good day" would be short-lived.

"Mama, are you okay?" I asked her when I saw her standing behind the stove, tears streaming down her face.

"I've lifted that pan a million times, why wouldn't I be able to do that now?" she asked amid sobs, and that was when I saw Maria on the floor, scooping up bits of egg and chorizo from the floor into a dustpan.

"It's okay, Mama," Maria said. "It's a heavy pan. Anyone could have dropped it."

I squatted down on the floor, taking the dustpan from Maria. "Hey, you shouldn't be down on the floor in your condition. I'll take care of this."

I helped Maria get back on her feet and watched with worry as she rubbed her distended belly after the effort.

That was when I caught the distraught look on my mother's face. She looked like a girl standing there looking at two of her grown children, her youngest child heavy with her grandchild.

"I-I-I'm tired," she said brokenly, and I had to swallow hard past the lump of emotion in my throat.

Maria grabbed my mother's hand. "Okay, Mama. It's okay. How about we get you settled in for a nap? It's been an exciting morning."

"I don't need naps—I'm not a child," she insisted as I finished cleaning up and dumped the dustpan's contents into the nearby garbage can.

I cleared my throat, "Actually, I think Maria could really use a nap before that baby gets here … Lord knows you won't be getting any once that little one is here," I said when Maria scoffed. I turned back to my mom. "Do you think maybe you could help her get settled in?"

My mother's eyes brightened. "He's right, Maria. You need to rest. C'mon," she said, grabbing her daughter's hand. "Let's get you all set up. I can even sing that song to you liked when you were little—you'll need to remember it for the baby." And with that, Mama was marching Maria away in hand just like when Maria was little.

Maria looked over her shoulder at me hesitantly, but I just shrugged my shoulders, feigning innocence.

"Oh, and Jaime, when you see your father, tell him to pick up some more eggs on the way home from work," Mama called out.

I grimaced but nodded obediently. "I'll do that, Mama."

Once I knew they were out of earshot, I pulled my phone from my back pocket and dialed a familiar number. It immediately went to voicemail. Sighing in frustration, I waited for the beep and said, "Silvia, this is your brother … not sure you would remember since you've been dodging me. Call me back. Please, or I'll be forced to come over there and embarrass you in front of your new girlfriend," I threatened. "Looooove you," I sang out to her before hanging up the phone.

Silvia and my mother had a complicated relationship. Since Mama became sick, Silvia had offered her support in the best way she thought possible: helping with the bills, paying the day nurse, and sending grocery orders. But she largely stayed away, and though part of me understood why, it was quickly becoming apparent the nurse and Maria would need more help, especially with Maria getting so far along in her pregnancy.

Silvia would have to face our mother whether she liked it or not, and unfortunately, I had to be the bad guy and convince her of that.

I let out a long breath and ventured back down the hall toward my mother's room. Peeking through the crack in the door, I smiled at what I saw. There was mother and daughter, sleeping peacefully in each other's arms just like when Maria was little.

Quietly, I padded back down the hall and slipped out of the house, letting the beautiful morning sun hit me in the face as I headed to my truck. Considering how late the bar stayed open, it was rare I was up and out this early, but after my night with Emma, I was running on adrenaline, so I figured I might as well get more eggs for my mom.

As I buckled my seatbelt, my phone buzzed in my pocket, and figuring it was Silvia, I pulled it out, bracing myself for her sharp reply. But it wasn't Silvia. Instead, it was a California number.

Emma: Hey, it's Emma. Not to sound to stalker-y, but I pulled your number from the employee directory. I wanted to make sure you had my number … for later. 🙂

I giggled like a schoolboy. I was thirty years old, and I was giggling in delight over an emoji from a girl I liked … maybe more than liked.

"Alright, Acosta, don't get ahead of yourself," I warned myself out loud as I cranked on the engine. I couldn't think of words like love, not yet anyway.

Going into work that evening, I couldn't fight back the grin that stretched across my face when my eyes fell on the barstool Emma had been perched on the night before.

I actually whistled as I prepared the bar for the evening. "Somebody seems extra chipper tonight," Charlie said with a sly smile as he rounded the tables.

I shrugged nonchalantly. Let Charlie work for it a bit. "I have no idea what you're talking about."

That was when Joey chimed in, "I'd be whistling, too, if I had a goddess like that looking at me with bedroom eyes," Joey said, drawing out the last two words dramatically.

"Bedroom eyes, huh?" Charlie asked with curiosity. "You holding out on me, bud?"

I shook my head, but Joey wasn't done. "Shit, you picked a hell of a night to be off, Charlie. They talked forever, and we were taking bets on how long before they just mauled each other." I scowled at Joey sharply in warning. He at least had the decency to look sheepish as he shrugged and said, "Sorry, boss, but it's true. There was something hot and heavy brewing."

Charlie laughed. "You're making it sound like he was having sex on the bar in front of everyone."

"He might as well have been. I'm man enough to admit I had to take a cold shower when I got home."

"Ugh," Charlie and I both said in unison.

Joey didn't seem embarrassed one bit, looking at me hesitantly before asking, "Is it true she's *the* heiress of Pine Crest Resorts?"

Charlie jerked toward me, alarm in his eyes. "Emma? You were with Emma last night?"

I smiled at him tightly, addressing Joey. "I need you to finish rolling that silverware before the party across the way wraps up. Shouldn't be much longer."

Joey looked between Charlie and me for a beat before nodding and excusing himself.

"Did I hear that right?" Charlie asked once Joey was out of earshot.

"He's making a bigger deal out of it than it is. We were just talking at the bar, catching up," I said, not really in the mood for Charlie's "realism" at the moment. He was my best friend, and I valued his opinion, but the guy was not the most positive person to talk to when it came to matters of the heart.

Charlie huffed out a laugh. "You know, everyone knows what an honest guy you are, but most don't realize it's because you're a shitty liar."

I could feel my jaw clench. "No offense, brother, but I don't need to defend who I spend my time with to you."

Charlie let out a frustrated sigh. "I get it. You're a grown man, and I'm not your keeper, but …" He trailed off, his face mottling with color.

"But what? Spit it out," I demanded, just wanting to get this over with.

He hesitated before saying, "I just want you to be careful. You remember last time …"

I laughed humorlessly, "Are you serious?"

Charlie put up a placating hand. "Maybe that was a poor choice of words. It's just … Look, I know a lot of time has passed, but she's still working for her old man, right?" he asked, letting the question hang in the air between us.

"What does that have to do with anything?"

"It has everything to do with it. She threw you over for the family business. Now she's well established in that business. If you weren't the first choice then, what makes you think you'll be the first choice now?"

I felt my hands clench at my sides, and never had a stronger urge to punch my best friend in the face than I did right then. He had no right to throw all these things in my face, and yet …

Yet they were all valid concerns. I just wasn't willing to let the euphoric bubble burst.

"Are you done?" I asked tersely.

Charlie scrubbed a frustrated hand over his face and let out a sigh. "Yeah, I guess I am."

"Good," I said, staring over his shoulder, not ready to look him in the eye and reveal my own reservations. "We need you behind the bar. It's getting backed up."

Charlie clucked his tongue and said begrudgingly, "Whatever you want, boss."

I shook my head because there was a chance I wouldn't get exactly what I wanted so badly.

Emma

"Well, hello, sunshine, nice of you to join the land of living," Caroline greeted me as I strolled to her table in The Lounge. "I hope you don't mind, but I already got us plates. I expected you to be famished after all your extracurricular activities," she said before taking another bite of her brunch.

I sat down in the chair across from her, busying myself with arranging my napkin on my lap. "I have no idea what you're talking about," I answered coyly before grabbing my fork because she was right—I was famished.

"Please, don't act like you haven't been having Olympic-style coitus with the hunky bartender of boyfriend's past for the past couple of days. How you're balancing that with your meetings and deadlines, I don't know, but I have to admit I'm feeling a tad neglected," she sniffed before shoving a smoothie bowl my way. "By the way, have you tried this? The server said they just added to the menu, and you could use the protein," she said, waggling her eyebrows suggestively.

I swallowed the bite of food I'd just taken, clearing my throat. "Really? You feel neglected?" I asked, disbelieving.

Caroline stuck out her bottom lip in a pout. "Of course," she said before taking a sip of her orange juice.

I huffed out a laugh. "I call bullshit. What's really bugging you?"

She chewed on her lip for a moment before relenting and saying, "Okay, fine, so I may not feel neglected … That's not really my style, and I'm more than capable of entertaining myself buuuut," she said drawing out the word. "I am a little hurt you're not sharing with your best friend. I'll have you know some of us are still in the middle of a sexual Sahara, and it's a little selfish of you to be bogarting all your juicy details."

I rolled my eyes at her, laughing. "What, you want me to draw you a picture?" I asked teasing.

Her eyes widened, "Only if you've invented some new position … then absolutely, yes." She laughed. "But c'mon, this is the guy you've been pining over for a decade—the one who got away. Now you've finally gotten to realize some of those fantasies, and that's no small thing. I mean, unless it is a small thing, and if so, then that's a bummer … or maybe that doesn't bother you. I don't know. Talk to meeee," she whined.

I burst out laughing. "Okay, okay. Without getting into too many details, I can tell you it's been … amazing. I mean, I know that sounds corny, but everything I imagined pales compared to what the last couple of days have been like."

Caroline let out a small squeal of excitement, thumping her hand on the table. "Ooh, I'm so excited for you. God, how awful would it have been to long for and wonder about someone for that long, and he turns out to be a dud in the sack?" she asked, shuddering in mock horror.

I shook my head. "You know it's not just about the sex. That connection is still there. I don't have to be anyone other than myself with him. I hate to say it, but as much as I'm enjoying myself, I'm a little scared. Oh, hell, who am I kidding? I'm a lot scared," I admitted.

Caroline nodded. "Afraid Daddy Moneybags will step in again?"

I nodded miserably.

Caroline sighed. "Look, I get how unpleasant he could make things for you, but what your father was threatening before isn't really a threat anymore, so what's stopping you other than the fear of family strife?"

"Strangely enough, it's still my mom. I know he can't take her away from me anymore, but he's been threatening to make changes to the company that would steer us away from her vision, not to mention the impact it would have on the employees that have become family to me.

The only reason he's kept a lot of the more tenured employees is because I keep reminding him how important loyalty was to Mom. But he keeps complaining they're expensive to keep around. And now this new merger …" I trailed off, knowing I was probably sharing way more details than the company would like, but this was Caroline. If there was anyone I could trust to be discrete, it was Caroline and Sophie.

"You still suspicious?" she pushed.

I nodded. "I'm still in talks with the son of Get Outdoors' CEO, and he keeps dropping hints that insinuate he's hoping for an additional "merger" if you know what I mean."

Caroline made a face. "Unfortunately, I know exactly what you mean. Have you told your father this guy is being a sleaze? I mean, your father is a lot of things, but I have a hard time believing he'd be okay with that kind of behavior."

I sighed. "That's why I'm confused. I update my father every day on our progress, and I've mentioned more than once this guy has other ideas that are less than professional, and he just tells me to keep an open mind, reminding me what a good family this guy comes from."

Caroline made another disgusted face. "Gross … and disappointing. My opinion of Daddy Moneybags is plummeting even further," she said before downing the last of her orange juice. "This conversation calls for something stronger. Excuse me, sir!" She called the attention of the waiter before ordering two mimosas.

I wouldn't normally day drink on a weekday, especially because I was supposed to meet with Andrew later in the day, but after the last couple of days, I figured my status quo lifestyle could benefit from a shakeup.

The server came back with our drinks, and Caroline savored a sip before sucking in a deep breath and saying, "Okay, now that I have some liquid courage in me, I'm just going to say it, Emma. I know how much this place means to you, and I know how much it meant to Mama Carter, but when is enough enough?"

"What do you mean?" I asked, a knot of dread forming in my chest.

Caroline eyed me warily. "You know exactly what I mean, Emma. Look, I know your father loves you in his own way, but he's been taking advantage of you for a really long time. Frankly, Sophie and I were concerned that once your mom passed away, he would take even more advantage of you. I think it's safe to say I don't think very highly of a man who uses his wife, his daughter's mother, against her to keep her in line. He's up to something, and I'm worried where that leaves you. Not to mention, this Andrew guy sounds sketchy as hell. I know how much you love this company and how much it meant to your mom, but is it really worth it?"

I could feel myself blanch at the question.

"You can't seriously be suggesting I just walk away from the company my family worked so hard to build? That I've been a part of since I was a child?" Even though I knew Caroline's heart was in my corner, her words still hurt.

She sighed. "I know it sounds insane to walk away, and it is, I get it. But you have so much to offer, and I don't think you're appreciated. Look, if it's a hell no, then the three of us will put our heads together, and we'll figure out a way to make this thing with your father work for you. But, Emma, we want you to be happy, and you've been unhappy for a really long time … even before your mom died."

I didn't respond for a moment, letting her words sink in. My knee-jerk reaction was to be furious at her suggestion, but she was my best friend who had only ever had my best interest at heart. Then Caroline said the words that would make the splinter in my heart dig in even deeper. "She would want you to do whatever it takes to be happy."

I couldn't look at Caroline then, not because I was mad at her but because she was speaking the truth.

My mom had been proud of what our family built, but she was even prouder to be my mom. I knew if I told her I wanted to join the circus, and she believed it would make happy, I would've had her full support.

What hurt more was I often wondered what my mom would have thought of everything that had happened since she'd died. I wondered if she was still proud—if she'd approve of how I'd chosen to live my life without her.

But what made it hurt even worse was the fact that I often wondered what my mom was thinking when she saw me from up there. I wondered if she was still proud, and I had to face the fact that she probably wouldn't like how I was handling things.

Caroline broke into my spiraling thoughts. "Hey, before you get lost in thinking you're somehow disappointing her, just stop. She adored you, and there's nothing you can do to change that fact. Sophie and I were always envious of your relationship with your mom. We would have killed to have that kind of support from our parents growing up. And I bet she'd have some choice words for your father regarding this whole merger fiasco."

That made me laugh because, as usual, she was right on the money. Caroline was an expert on reading people. "I just think she wouldn't want you to get so wrapped up in everything your dad wants or fighting him at every turn. There's more to life than world domination. She'd want you to enjoy your life—and that includes life *outside* of work. That's why I'm so glad you reconnected with Jaime. I admit I was a little worried at first, but it seems like things are going well?"

I couldn't help the smile that spread across my face. "Yeah, I'm not really sure where it's headed, but I'm trying to just be in the moment with him."

Caroline nodded her head in approval. "Well, then, let's raise a glass," she said, raising her champagne flute, "To staying in the moment and not allowing any jack-asses to ruin them."

We laughed as we clinked our glasses together, and I was so grateful she was there. Otherwise, I would've spun out over what was going to happen next, and for once in my life, I wanted to go with the flow and have fun.

And I had a hell of a lot of fun with Jaime, not to mention how comforting it was to just be in his presence. I felt at peace around him, and despite my best efforts, I couldn't help but wonder what the future held for us. If he even wanted a future with me.

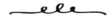

Yet another meeting with Andrew and more stalling. We got as far as agreeing on the location of the boutique onsite where we would offer their services, but then Andrew got distracted and seemed determined to take me out for a tour ... of my own hometown. He swore he'd run into a local who showed him some spots even I wouldn't know about.

I gritted my teeth and gave a tight smile. I seriously doubted his claim, and I couldn't help but bristle at the presumption when he slid his hand around my waist, trying to pull me in closer as he tried to sweet talk me into spending the afternoon with him.

"Look, Andrew, I appreciate you taking the time to experience the grandeur that is Silverpine. Believe me, you'll find no bigger fan of this town than me. But we have business to tend to," I reminded him, gently pushing him away so he understood I was done playing games.

He gave me an oily smile that had my posture stiffening defensively. "Come on, you can't be like this all the time. All work and no play makes Jane a dull girl," he ribbed, and I resisted the urge to throat punch him.

I gave him a smile that more closely resembled a grimace as I told him, "Indeed, it does, Mr. Travers," I bit off. "But work comes before play, and I know our fathers are quite eager for us to settle this deal."

"You don't know the half of it," he said, and alarm bells went off in my head.

"I don't? Then please, enlighten me."

Andrew looked like he'd been caught sharing too much, then laughed it off. "I just mean those two have gotten their heads together and seem to have some specific ideas about what needs to happen here. I can't say they're bad ideas. We just have to get everyone on board," he said.

"You don't know the half of it," I muttered, parroting him, not wanting to continue this cat-and-mouse game any longer.

I looked at him for a long moment, trying to decide what my next move was. I'd never had this much trouble with a potential client—and I'd never disliked one so intensely.

At his core, Andrew was an overgrown child, but he had a greasiness about him that set me on edge. It didn't help there were a million other things I'd rather do with my time than babysit him.

"Listen, I think we made good progress today settling on the location for the boutique. Why don't we call it a day, and you can continue exploring Silverpine? I have a friend visiting, and I would like to show her around town."

"Oh, well, there you go. Why don't you and her join my little tour—we can make it a threesome," he said, grinning, and I cringed at the way he emphasized that last word.

My smile was turning into a baring of teeth, and I could feel it. I sucked in a deep breath, trying to compose myself. "Actually, it's a girls' day out, sorry."

He nodded, still leering at me, but I was already moving toward the exit.

"I'll be in touch to arrange another meeting. Hopefully, we'll be a little more productive next time, and Andrew,"

I said before turning away, "Please be prepared with those figures. It would be really helpful in determining staffing needs so we can begin recruiting." With that, I waved to him and headed toward the elevator.

The lobby of Pine Crest was turning into a heaven and hell situation for me. The meetings I had to endure with Andrew in The Lounge were exhausting while the dimly lit bar featuring Jaime instantly put me at ease … and excited me.

I'd been pondering whether I was just trying to re-capture my younger days, but there was nothing childish about what was happening between Jaime and me. Any sense of decorum I had went out the window when he was around, and I couldn't keep my hands to myself. Thankfully, he was more than receptive.

Even if we didn't have sex, getting to touch him had become vital to my ability to get through the day. It hadn't even been a week, and yet so much had changed. I had changed. I couldn't help but worry about how it would hurt like hell when I returned to California.

Damn it, Emma. Remember what you told Caroline.

I sucked in a deep breath as the elevator rose to the top floor.

Stay in the moment. Take it one day at a time. You don't know what the future holds.

I didn't know why I was torturing myself. There was nothing that could keep me away from Jaime at this point, so why fight it?

I walked down the hall to my suite, remembering the last time I was with Jaime. How I'd woken up to him trailing kisses down my jaw and neck, tickling the sensitive skin of my neck with his scruffy beard. I could get used to that wake-up call every day.

With that memory fresh in my head, I pulled out my phone to call Jaime to see what he was doing. Maybe I could sneak in a quick visit with him before he had to work. I didn't care where or how—like an addict, I just needed to feel his touch.

His voice was deep and sexy when he answered the phone. "Hello?"

A shiver ran through me, landing squarely between my thighs. "Well, hello to you, too," I said a little breathlessly.

He chuckled softly. "Sorry, I just woke up."

"I hope I didn't wake you?" I was still wrapping my head around his schedule since he worked late and slept in the morning.

"No, I was awake. Just lying here thinking about a certain redhead."

I took the bait. "Who is she? Do I need to hunt her down?"

He laughed a little louder. "Bella, you must know by now. There's only one redhead for me."

A warmth spread through my chest, even as his words scared the hell out of me.

It made me think of a future, of a time when I would never have to leave his side again. But I didn't know if that was possible in the real world. Right now, we were living in a fairytale, and I didn't want it to end.

"I better be," I teased him. "I did have a reason for calling … I wanted to see if you had a little time before work. Maybe we could go for a walk? Or grab a quick bite to eat? Doesn't have to be anything big."

"Actually, I have the night off."

I was thirty years old, and I felt like a kid who'd just been told I was going to Disneyland. "Oh, then you must have plans already," I baited him.

"I certainly do. Remember that redhead I told you about? I was thinking of taking her to a lavish dinner, followed by a decadent dessert …"

Excitement ran through me at the suggestion.

"That is, if you're not too busy with important business meetings with successful, rich suitors," he said jovially enough, but there was an edge to it.

"No, thank God. I am free … and all yours. Just let me know when to be ready."

"I'll pick you up at six. Dress comfortably—and not fancy Carter comfortably. Emma, the girl I grew up with comfortably, okay?"

I smiled, knowing exactly what he meant, and it thrilled me he knew what that meant.

He remembered young Emma's t-shirts and shorts with hiking boots. He had no expectation for the woman in the high-end sporting apparel that was expected of her by her clients.

I let out a satisfied sigh. "Got it. I'll see you soon."

"Bye, Emma," he said, and I could hear the smile in his voice and the promise of what was to come later.

I was going to spend the evening with Jaime Acosta, and I was positively giddy.

But my excitement was immediately extinguished by the shrill ring of my phone, which was still in my hand.

It was my father.

He was probably just checking in for a report on how the negotiations were going, but I dreaded having to tell him Andrew was stalling, and I was struggling to figure out what his angle was other than trying to cop a feel at every opportunity.

I sucked in a steadying breath and answered. "Hey, Dad, how's it going?"

"That's exactly what I'd like to know from you, young lady," he said harshly, and any remaining relaxed feeling rushed out of me.

I hesitated before answering. "Well, I'll be honest, things are beyond frustrating on the business front."

"But, from what I hear, not on the personal front. *Things* seem to be going well for you, which is probably why you haven't been able to close this deal," he sniped.

"Dad? I don't follow. What are you talking about?"

"You forget, Emma, Silverpine is a small town—much of which I own, and people talk. Plus, I still have some faithful employees at the resort. Why am I hearing rumors you're sneaking around with the help?"

A thousand shades of red appear before my eyes. "I'm sorry, did you say 'the help'?" My father was old-fashioned, but that expression was so disrespectful. I was livid.

"You know," he fumed, "I had reservations about hiring that boy again, but he blew the other candidates away with glowing recommendations and a reputation as someone who could turn that bar around. I should've known he was just trying to get in my daughter's pants again."

Fury washed through me. "Father," I said forcefully. "You are way out of line. I don't know what you've heard or who's reporting on me, but might I remind you I am a grown ass woman, and who I choose to spend my time with is none of your business."

"The hell it isn't. Your mother and I worked entirely too hard to set you up in such a sweet position for you to throw it all away on some penniless boy with an inferior upbringing."

"Dad!"

"No, l wouldn't let you waste your time with that bum back then, and I'm certainly not going to allow you to spend time with a man whose best quality is getting people drunk with fancy cocktails. You need to keep your eye on the prize. If you're so hard up for male attention, why don't you play ball with Andrew Jr.?"

I huffed out of a disbelieving laugh. "Are you serious right now? You're upset about my reputation being compromised by someone I've known and trusted most of my life, who has grown into a kind, mature man? And instead, you'd rather pawn me off on a sleazy, ill-mannered man-child just because he has money?"

"That's always been your problem, Emma. You're close minded. You haven't even bothered to get to know him. I can assure you he has more positive qualities than you're giving him credit for."

"I've gotten to know him as much as necessary to conduct business. What do you suggest? I shack up with him?"

"Please, Emma," he hissed out. "There's no need to be crude. It wouldn't be the worst thing in the world to consort with your own kind."

Bile rose in my throat, and I wanted to throw my phone across the room as hard as I could and shatter it into a million pieces.

Just when I thought it couldn't get worse, my father continued. "Emma, I need you to understand I just want what's best for you, and a bartending Spaniard isn't it."

A thousand ugly words bubbled up on my tongue, and yet they were frozen in my throat.

"And I imagine your mother wouldn't be enthralled with your behavior, either. In fact, I think she'd be down-right embarrassed."

How dare he?

By the time my response finally arranged itself in my brain and I was ready to speak, he had moved on, talking to his secretary. "Emma, I have urgent business I need to tend to, but you need to get your act together. Otherwise, I'll have to come down there and finish the deal myself. And if I have to come down there, that boy toy of yours can forget about having gainful employment—not just at the resort but anywhere in town."

And then silence. No goodbye, he just hung up.

I stared down at my darkened phone in shock, shaking all over.

All those suspicions I'd had about my dad, all the concerns Sophie and Caroline had been cautiously laying out for me, were now undeniable. The father I knew was gone. Whatever tolerance or compassion he possessed died with my mother.

I wanted to scream out in frustration but didn't want to alarm the other guests. Instead, I gritted my teeth and dialed a familiar number. "Hey, I need you," I said, skipping a formal greeting.

The voice on the other end didn't question it. They just said they'd meet me in five. And less than five minutes later, Caroline was at my door, looking uneasy and ready to throw down my behalf.

As soon as she saw me, her eyes widened. "Whoa, Daddy Moneybags really stepped in it, didn't he? Or was it Jaime? Do I need to kill him? That would be so inconvenient, but I'll do what needs to be done."

I shook my head. "It's not Jaime, but your first guess was right on the money."

Her lips pressed together in a grimace. "Do I need to call Sophie?"

I hesitated. I would love nothing more than to have a powwow with both of them right now, but I didn't want to bother Sophie when she was working.

"No, I don't want to disturb her in the middle of the day. I just need to walk this off. Do you want to go on a little hike with me?"

Caroline blinked at me slowly. "As in out in the woods?"

I gave her a hopeful smile. "It'll make me feel better."

She let out a long sigh. "Fine, I'll go change my shoes. But for the record, I'm the superior friend for hiking in the woods for you."

I laughed as I shut the door behind me, then followed her to her room so she could retrieve her running shoes. "You know, you might actually like it if you give it a chance. Besides, when you hear about what my father just said to me, I don't think you'll even notice we're outdoors, which is a pity."

She looked at me expectantly. "Well, don't let me leave in suspense. I'd say I don't have all day, but we both know I do," she said, giving me a teasing smile.

Thankfully, Caroline was equal parts appalled and supportive as I shared the latest despicable exchange with my father, and I felt renewed by the time we came back from our hike ... though Caroline looked a little worse for the wear after communing with the great outdoors.

"Where are we going, Jaime?" I asked late that night.

He smiled at me wickedly. "Patience, Bella."

I was tired from the emotionally and physically draining day, but I couldn't imagine being anywhere else than with Jaime, even if he was taking us to a dark, secluded area.

We started the night with a lavish dinner—just as he'd promised me—at Mabel's. It was definitely a trip down memory lane to be seated in the booth across from Jaime again. It almost felt like the younger version of him was sitting across from me, and yet I was delighted with the new manlier version, too.

I did my best to push the conversation with my father out of my head. When I'd told Caroline I planned to spend the evening with Jaime, she'd coached me to just enjoy the evening and not let my dad ruin anything else.

"Emma, it's one thing when a father gets involved in his eighteen-year-old daughter's life. Parents want to protect their kids from the mistakes they need to make and learn from. He may have had good intentions back then, but this latest stunt feels like a power play. He's trying to control you," Caroline said cautiously. "You're thirty years old. You negotiate multi-million-dollar mergers and manage a team of people who depend on you, and you do so with tenacity and grace. The fact that he still treats you like a child is more than worrisome. He has no right to tell you who you can and can't spend time with. And that little dig about your mother being embarrassed by your behavior? I hope her ghost haunts his ass relentlessly. Karma's a bitch."

Despite the seriousness of her expression, I'd laughed at that.

"I'm serious," Caroline said, "I realize Mama Carter is probably way too sweet for that, but if there was ever a time for her to roll over in her grave and start putting the fear of God in your father, it would be going after her baby girl like this."

Maybe it was wrong that I found Caroline's anger on my behalf so comforting, but it made me realize how much Caroline, Sophie, and I had acted like pseudo-mothers for one another. In times of need, we were more than just best friends and soul sisters. Very often we were the parents each other needed because our actual parents weren't capable.

"Come on. You have to recognize some of this," Jaime said, breaking into my thoughts.

I tried to decipher landmarks around me, but it wasn't until we drove around a curve and I saw a cabin in the distance that it started clicking together. "The lake?"

He smiled at me. "I can't believe you don't remember."

I laughed. "Please, you think I forgot about the lake? It's just so dark out here, and I'm so used to the light pollution in LA—I'm having a hard time getting my eyes to adjust in the dark. If you brought me out here during the day, I would've known right away," I said, directing my gaze out through the windshield to take in the landscape.

Silver Lake was where Jaime and I would meet up in secret when we were kids. I would sneak out of my bedroom window and walk a few blocks before he would pick me up so my parents wouldn't hear the starting of his truck.

Ironically, Jaime still had that same truck, and I'd felt like a teenager again as he pulled through the clearing close to the edge of the lake.

I smiled when I saw the familiar dock and looked back at Jaime's sexy profile. "Yeah," I whispered. "I remember this all too well." He had no idea I'd visited this place in my mind countless times over the years. That it had served as a refuge when things were hard and the sorrowful reminder of what might've been.

He looked at me then, his eyes shining with a small smile playing at his lips. "Shall we?"

I resisted the urge to launch myself across the bench seat of the truck and kiss him. I could sense he was going for a moment, and while I wanted to feel his lips on mine, I pushed it aside. "Let's do it."

He got out of the driver's side of the truck, grabbing something from the backseat before coming around to my side, opening the door, and offering me his hand.

I took it, climbing down from the passenger seat, and followed him to our spot next to the pier. It was chilly, but Jaime had grabbed a blanket and laid it out on the ground.

I'd followed his instructions from our call earlier and wore an old, worn-out Stanford t-shirt and comfy jeans. No corporate Emma in sight.

I sat down on the blanket as he settled down beside me, stretching out his long legs next to my shorter ones, his shoulder bumping against mine and sending sparks of pleasure through me. Only he could make me so excited just from the bump of a shoulder.

"I know it's not quite the same," he said, "but I couldn't resist."

"Say no more," I reassured him. It had been a special spot for us growing up. It held all our secrets from years past: how I worried my father would send me far away after high school when I just wanted to stay close to the place and people I loved. How Jaime wasn't sure what he wanted to do, but he knew it wasn't construction like his father. I didn't know then my worst fears would come true, and I would lose Jaime.

I didn't notice when he put his arm around me, but I felt Jaime stiffen in question as a fresh wave of anger at my father's words from earlier washed over me. "Emma? Are you okay? You got tense all of a sudden."

I shook my head. "Yeah, I'm fine. Just stupid stuff from work, but I don't want that ruining our evening."

He shook his head. "But something is bothering you. Is it the guy you've been meeting with? Is he making you uncomfortable?" he questioned, and I look up at him, confused.

I'd mentioned Andrew could get a little handsy but had left it at that. "Why would you think that?"

"My employees see things in The Lounge, and they talk. One server said he's a sleazeball, flirting with the female staff and making them feel uneasy. He flirts with guests, too. I'm just worried about you having to meet with him so frequently. You know, if he oversteps, you just have to call. And if I'm not there, Charlie will gladly put him in his place."

I laughed. "Jaime, I appreciate the offer, but I'm a grown woman, and I can handle Andrew. I don't need to be rescued."

"I know," he said. "That doesn't mean I won't want to."

I smiled and leaned in to kiss him. It was nice to have somebody who wanted to rescue you, even if you didn't need it.

After I kissed him softly, I pulled back and said, "Thank you for wanting to take care of me, Jaime. It means a lot."

He wasn't ready to let go of the subject just yet. "Emma? What's the nature of this deal? I understand if you can't tell me, but why does this guy think it's okay to be so aggressive, and why is your father allowing it?"

I barked out a laugh. "I can't begin to comprehend why my father does anything. Just when I think I've figured him out, he surprises me," I said bitterly.

"Surprises you? Or disappoints you?" Jaime said, hitting the nail on the head because, deep down, his behavior really wasn't surprising to me.

He'd threatened to take away the most important person in my life if I didn't break off all communication with Jaime all those years ago. And my best friends had been warning me for years my father was only out for himself and wouldn't hesitate to throw me under if it suited him.

But I didn't want to believe it. I was his only child—the only family he had left. I couldn't believe he would be so cold and calculating.

I pulled away from Jaime, and he was quick to come after me. "Hey, I'm not trying to bring up old stuff. I'm just worried," he clarified.

I shook my head. "No, you have every right to feel the way you do about my father. I just haven't decided how I feel about him yet," I said wryly. "Kind of pathetic, huh? I'm a master of getting to know people, finding out what makes them tick so I can close the deal, and yet the person I'm supposed to know better than anyone, I can't see. Considering your history with him, you must think I'm an idiot, and I wouldn't blame you for it. "

Jaime reached out his hand, cupped my cheek, and ran the pad of his thumb over my skin as I lean into his touch. "I've never thought you're an idiot. You're intensely loyal, and that's something I've always loved about you. But I would be lying if I said I didn't wonder what life would've been like if …" He trailed off.

"If what?" I asked, knowing the answer would probably hurt but needing to hear it anyway.

He averted his eyes. "If your loyalty extended to those outside your immediate family," he admitted, and it felt like a punch to the gut. "I don't blame you for having an intense loyalty to your family."

"You sure about that?" I asked, desperate to know.

"No, Emma, I don't. I just … it's hard to see those closest to you for who they are, no matter how brilliant you are. Instinctively, we want to give our family members the benefit of the doubt. I watched how your father treated his family, only to have you forgive him for his misdeeds time and time again. And I resented the hell out of him. But never you. I knew you were in an impossible position."

Sadly, Jaime didn't know the half of it. He had no idea my father had threatened to keep my mother away from me. She'd just gotten sick, and he was going to send her away under the guise of getting her the best treatment money could buy. I couldn't stand the thought of being separated from her, especially as she fought her first bout of cancer.

If I she hadn't gotten sick, maybe I would have been with Jaime this whole time—I would have had the courage to choose him, but that wasn't the choice I was given.

Jaime was an intelligent man, an old soul who innately understood life was full of challenges and heartache. I guess I'd hoped his understanding would keep him from feeling hurt. He was so angry with me back then, and it occurred to me now that was his way of expressing his heartbreak.

"Emma?" he prodded gently.

I smiled at him sadly. "I hate that his actions have affected you," I admitted. It was hard to get the words out after all these years. "I just figured it was better to make a clean break, that you were better off without all the drama," I whispered, unable to say the words any louder.

Even in the dark, I could see Jaime shaking his head, a wry twist to his lips. "Seriously? You thought I would be better off without you?"

I hesitated, before I said, "Well, no, I guess I thought you would be better off without the mess that is … my family."

"You mean your father," he clarified, and I nodded, even though there was no point.

My mother had embraced just about everybody she'd met, and she'd always liked Jaime. But she'd also felt obligated to stand by her husband and his wishes. Still, I wonder what she would've thought if she'd known how her husband leveraged my love for her to get me away from Jaime.

"I would have taken you any way I could, mess and all," he said with a grin. "Besides, every family is a mess. You would've had to deal with my hotheaded Hispanic family." We watched each other for a long moment. "Look," he finally said. "We can rehash the past, but it doesn't change any of it. The only thing we have control over is what's in front of us, and I'm pretty excited about what's in front of me," he said, closing his arms around me from behind and nuzzling my neck.

We stayed like that for a long time, my head leaning back against his strong shoulder, inhaling the scent of him while we looked up at the stars.

This was heaven. If someone told me a couple of weeks ago that I'd be in Jaime Acosta's arms, feeling desired and cared for, I would have laughed my ass off. But now that I was here, it felt like the universe conspired to make sure the two of us were in this place at that exact moment.

I dared to shut my eyes, closing out the stars and just inhaling the scent of Jaime.

"I've been thinking," Jaime said, "would you like to come to dinner on Sunday with the family?"

My heart kicked into overdrive. I'd met his family before, but this felt like a big step. What would they think was going on between us if he brought me home? We haven't even defined what this was yet. But as doubts swirled in my head, my heart was thrilled he asked.

"Are you sure that's a good idea?"

He laughed. "I know they can be a lot to handle…"

"No, Jaime, that's not what I meant …" I trailed off, not knowing how to finish that statement.

I let the words hang there until Jaime answered, "I think it's a great idea." I could hear the stubbornness in his voice.

"Besides, we're kind of reinstating the ritual Sunday family dinner. Silvia hasn't come around much lately, and Maria and I are hoping to reconcile her with our mother."

I remembered Silvia. She'd always been strong willed and very independent, and butted heads with their mother, so I wasn't surprised to hear they weren't on great terms. Although I wondered how Silvia could stay away, knowing time with their mother was limited.

"It's complicated," Jaime continued. "But I don't want Silvia to regret …" He trailed off, but I knew what he was thinking—not making amends before his mom passed away.

"I understand. There's nothing worse than all the things left unsaid."

He paused for a moment before he asked, "Did you leave a lot of things unsaid with your mom?"

I thought about it for a moment. At the time, I hadn't, so I answered honestly, "No, my mom and I were at peace with one another before she died. Of course, we'd always been close. I can't remember ever fighting with her."

And that was the truth. We were unusually close for mother and daughter, even when I was a hormonal teenager. Most of my angst was directed toward my father.

Somehow, until I'd met Jaime, I'd always felt like it was my mom and me against the world.

"There's a lot I've wanted to tell her since, though. It would be really nice to have her guidance."

Jaime looked at me and then gazed up at the stars. "Who says you can't still get her guidance? It might just come in another form."

I looked at him, smiling. "You always were a wise old man in a young man's body."

He laughed. "Shower me with compliments all you want, but you still haven't answered my question."

I didn't let myself overthink it and answered from my heart, "Yes, I'll go to Sunday dinner with your family … as long as you promise I won't be intruding."

He laughed. "Come on, Emma. You know it's a revolving door over there," he teased. "And you're welcome at my home anytime."

I reached for him and brought his mouth to mine, sealing his declaration with a kiss.

There was so much about this that felt confusing, and yet everything finally made sense for the first time in a very long time. I didn't want to overthink it. I just wanted to feel his lips on mine and the rest of me as he leaned me back against the ground, lowering my head and kissing me passionately.

We were finally going to do something I'd dreamed about for years. I would finally get to make love to Jaime beneath the stars in our favorite place—a place where a thousand promises and secrets still existed.

Jaime

Having Emma in my arms at our sacred spot made all my boyhood fantasies pale in comparison.

Maybe I should've taken her back to the truck—at least there was the bench seat to lie on—but it seemed fitting that we christen the spot where so many memories had been made.

I could sense Emma's conflict, but we'd fallen back into our old habits. Talking and laughing and just enjoying each other, but when I brought up anything relating to the future, I could see a shadow cast over her expression.

I didn't want to push her too hard, too fast because, despite her recent revelations about her father, her life was still very much intertwined with his. He was the only family she had, and I could see her wrestling with what she wanted now that she was accepting the truth about him.

I suspect John Carter's feelings about me hadn't changed, so my fate was in her hands. I was determined to hang onto her, to make her see how amazing her future could be—if she'd just chose me.

That was why I brought her to the lake. I knew I'd fallen in love with her the second I saw her, but I was fairly certain it was our trips to the lake, looking up at the stars, that made Emma finally fall for me.

When I first returned to Pine Crest, I'd come out here with a six-pack of beer and let myself wallow in my memories. But now … now I was back in the arms of the woman I loved, and I was going to savor the moment.

Her wet kisses became more demanding, and I'd never been more grateful that I'd thought ahead and brought a blanket. I shifted my weight, settling in next to her, and a thrill shot through me at her moan of protest.

"Just changing positions, Bella. I want better access to this gorgeous body," I said, sitting up and encouraging her to straddle my lap.

She gave me a slow grin as she ground her heat against me and kissed me again, moaning against my lips.

I ran my fingers through her hair and down her back, slipping them around her waist, pulling up her t-shirt so we could be skin on skin.

"I can't tell you how many times I dreamed about taking you here," I whispered against her mouth as I helped her out of her shirt, my hands immediately unhooking her bra.

I slipped the straps off her shoulders and marveled at her magnificent breasts. That hadn't gotten old, and I didn't think it ever would. I clutched her to me, burying my face in her neck and showering her with kisses, enjoying the way her fingers dug into my hair and massaged my scalp.

"I'm thinking about as often as I've dreamed about you here," she answered breathlessly as my mouth found a nipple and sucked it in between my lips, teasing it with my tongue and teeth.

She let out a cry, and her hips worked against my hardness again, coaxing a growl from my throat. I needed her as close as I could get, but I also enjoyed teasing her entirely too much.

"I'm sorry it took so long," she whispered, and I could hear the sorrow in her voice.

That made me stop, and I pulled my head away from her so I could look into her eyes. "You don't need to be sorry about anything, Emma."

She huffed out a laugh. "You sure about that? I mean, I was the one who …"

"Emma, no," I insisted. "You were forced to choose, and you did what you thought was best. Don't get me wrong, it hurt like hell, but I understand why you did what you did."

Over the last few days, I'd seen the weight of the guilt she carried, and while her betrayal will always exist between us, every new memory we make eases the pain in my heart.

"Besides," I teased, "maybe it's a blessing we didn't get to experience this with each other until now. I actually know what the hell I'm doing."

She giggled. "You *certainly* do."

"Be glad you never had to experience the fumbling hands of my teenage self," I said, leaning in to kiss her neck.

She said her next words so softly I almost didn't hear them. "I would've loved that, too."

I knew she was speaking the truth, but I didn't want to think about it too much because it stabbed at an old wound that remained unhealed. The same wound that had me fantasizing about hunting down John Carter over the years and making him pay for what he'd stripped away from both of us.

Determined to distract the sadness away, I urged her to stand so I could drag her jeans and panties down before quickly disrobing myself.

Then she was straddling me again, our mouths fused together, and I let out a moan at the feeling of her wetness against my erection.

God, I needed to be inside her.

Would that sense of urgency ever go away? Of not surviving one more breath if I wasn't surrounded by her warmth, her love?

I was embarrassed to say there was little foreplay, but it didn't seem to matter. We just needed to be joined together. Without prompting, Emma rose on her knees and positioned me at her opening before saying, "Jaime, I need you. I can't wait."

"Wait. What about protection?" I asked.

"I'm on the pill … and I really want to feel you. All of you. With nothing in between us."

She didn't have to say another word. I urged her down over me, and she seated herself on my cock, letting out a long moan. Once I was buried deep inside her, I let her set the rhythm, reveling in the way those lips breathed out pleas and sighs of pleasure as her pussy spasmed around me.

It wasn't just sex—it was the joining of two souls who had been separated for far too long, reunited at the spot where it all began.

I could tell she was getting close because she was grinding on me hard, sliding her tight channel up and down my shaft, making me cry out. "Fuck, Emma, that's my girl. Keep going, come for me," I coached her until her fingers dug into my shoulders, and she cried out my name.

Her orgasm radiated through her as she continued rocking her hips, encouraging my release. I came hard inside her, groaning out, "Fuck, yes. Your pussy is so fucking perfect. I can't get enough, baby."

The next thing I knew, her mouth was on me, and we were lying in the dirt kissing for what seemed like an eternity before she pulled back and looked down fiercely into my eyes. "Jaime," she pleaded, "make love to me again."

As I gazed into her eyes, I knew I couldn't deny her. I just hoped she'd let me prove that to her for the rest of our lives.

The following days were a bit nerve-racking. I was in seventh heaven during my stolen moments with Emma, but I couldn't help but feel the stress emanating from her. I chalked it up to nerves about coming to Sunday dinner.

It wasn't that my mother disliked Emma. When we were younger, she'd loved having Emma over to the house, but my mother had a sixth sense for people, and she'd known before it became an issue that John Carter would intervene.

I had been young and brash enough to brush off her concerns, even though she'd tried to tell me as diplomatically as possible that people like Mr. Carter didn't like their offspring mixing with people not of the same breed. Whether she'd meant because we were immigrants or Spanish or poor, I was never completely sure. But she'd been certain he would cause trouble.

Meanwhile, I'd thought love could conquer anything.

When everything went down with her father and Emma made her choice, I'd come home to my mother and at first didn't want to share anything because I'd figured she would gloat. But she'd taken one look at my heartbroken face, clucked her tongue, and said "Oh, mijo," and the next thing I knew, I was in my mother's embrace, crying my eyes out.

She'd never said, "I told you so." She'd let me mope what she believed was an appropriate amount of time before encouraging me to get out there and experience life.

Still, when I'd decided to leave Silverpine, she hadn't been very happy about it. When she'd told me to get out there and experience life, she didn't mean leaving the town limits, and I'd always wondered if she'd blamed Emma for that.

Emma having dinner with the family wasn't the only thing making me nervous. I pulled my truck in front of the Bank of Silverpine and sucked in a deep breath before climbing out and squaring my shoulders. I had a different battle to fight today that had nothing to do with Emma, but still concerned our upcoming family dinner, and I wasn't looking forward to it.

As I walked through the doors, my eyes immediately found the familiar face of my oldest sister. She was just finishing with a customer, smiling professionally, but as her eyes scanned the lobby and landed on me, her smile dropped, and her posture tensed.

"God give me strength," I muttered to myself as I marched over to Silvia. "Hey, sis. You've been dodging my calls."

She sniffed. "I haven't been dodging, Jaime. I'm just simply not answering. Why are you here? Are the deposits not going through?" she asked, referring to her weekly contribution to Mom's account to help pay for the at-home nurse and any other essentials she might need.

"Nope, they're arriving like clockwork," I said. "But you know that's not why I'm here." I hesitated before diving in. "Maria and I want to bring back our Sunday dinner tradition."

"Oh, God," Silvia groaned.

I pressed on, undeterred by her antics. "And it's not Sunday dinner without all of us there."

She leveled me with an annoyed stare. "I'm pretty sure your mama would disagree if she could remember."

I let out a frustrated sigh. "Silvia, I know things have been rocky between you and Mama. I get it. But ... we're running out of time, and this has to stop. I don't want you to live with regrets after she's gone. You need to make peace. Soon."

Silvia cocked a brow, her nostrils flaring in anger. "You think I don't know that? I think about it every day. You make it sound so easy ... like I can just go over there and play nice. You, of all people, should know it's never that easy with Mama. She really hurt me, and every time I try to gather up the courage to see her, it just … I'm just reminded it's going to be another heartbreak."

I sighed. I felt for her I really did, but time was running out.

There were more bad days than good, and that metaphorical hourglass has become more insistent—the sand slipping through faster than any of us expected. Maria and I worried about them never mending things before Mama passed.

For her part, Maria had been trying to get through to our sister. But being the baby of the family, Silvia easily pushed her aside, no matter how much Maria begged. But I was her big brother, and our father had deemed me the man of the house before he'd died, so I was hoping to God I would have some sway in the situation.

"Silvia, I can't force you to be there although I'm tempted to just throw you in a potato sack and drag your ass there kicking and screaming just put an end to this stupid thing, but I won't do that," I said after she gave me a look that told me she would murder me first. "Time is running out, Silvia. I'm not misleading you or exaggerating. You need to decide what you can live with, and you need to figure it out soon," I told her before turning on my heel and storming out of the bank.

When I got behind the wheel of my truck, I let out a frustrated growl. She could be so stubborn. I understand she was hurt, but the stakes were too high.

My frustration, however, melted away when I saw a text from Emma.

Emma: I can't stop thinking about you. ▢

I grinned, feeling like a boy again before texting back.

Jaime: Naughty thoughts, I hope …

Emma: Of course. I was just thinking about that old truck of yours …

Jaime: What about it?

Emma: I can't believe you still have it. I thought for sure I'd lose my virginity in that truck.

Jaime: Really? I wish I knew that back then—you definitely could have had your way with me.

Emma: Lol. I've never had sex in a vehicle before … want to take my virginity, so to speak?

Jaime: Tell me more.

Emma: I'm getting wet just thinking about it … thinking we might get caught, so I try to stay quiet, but soon, I can't take it anymore, and I'm screaming your name while I come all over your cock.

Holy shit. Her fantasy had me swallowing hard and shifting in my seat, trying to ease the ache from my growing erection. I glanced around the cab of the very truck she was referring to and grinned like an idiot. I was the luckiest son of a bitch in the world—dirty talking

Emma had my full attention. But what was even better was knowing she'd fantasized about me over the years, and it was a shot to the heart and groin. All this time I'd wondered if she'd thought about me the same way I did her, and now … I was a man on a mission.

Jaime: I can't think of anything better than feeling you wrapped around me in this truck, screaming my name. There's no sweeter sound than you losing control just for me. Promise me you'll lose control with me and let me inside in all the ways.

Her reply was one word, but it was one word that wrapped around me and worked to fill in all the cracks in my heart.

Emma: Promise.

And that started an afternoon-long text exchange.

I love days like that, where we were still connected, even when we couldn't be together, and her messages comforted me knowing I was still on her mind.

What I didn't love was her having to deal with that prick business associate I'd been hearing rumors about.

It wasn't just the man I was hearing rumors about, but the entire company he was a part of. One server, Susan, informed me his company was known for land acquisition, and she asked me nervously, "You don't think they're trying to buy the land behind the resort, do you?"

The people of Silverpine never wanted to see that land sold off. We appreciated the revenue the resort brought in and the jobs that were created, but expansion would give us over to pure commercialism. We were proud of our lack of strip malls and big box stores.

If there was anything most Coloradans were familiar with, it was the term "land acquisition" and how it often led to the destruction of the surrounding beauty.

Silverpine managed to avoid capitalistic takeovers, thanks in large part to Lydia Carter and now Emma, who was honoring her mother's wishes.

But I didn't like the rumors I was hearing.

Susan continued with bated breath, "Get Outdoors did the same thing in Alaska, apparently. There was this town that held out even longer than we have. Then the Travers' came in and, within months, flattened everything. Now they have a bunch of steel storage container-looking buildings, a McDonald's and Starbucks, and all the wildlife has run off."

I was a little taken aback when Susan's eyes turned to me, pleading. "Jaime, everybody knows you've been hanging around Emma Carter. Maybe you can find out for us."

Trying to reassure my staff, "Look, I've lived in Silverpine for a long time. Every few years, there's some threat of impending development, and every time, it gets shut down. Let's not make things worse by giving into the hysteria of the rumors."

Emma didn't say much, but I knew the deal was weighing heavily on her, and yet I hadn't asked her about it. I didn't want to ruin our time together by talking about work or the family business.

Besides, at that moment, I had more pressing matters—namely, how I was going to juggle a family dinner with an old flame and my bitter oldest sister.

When I picked up Emma, she was a bundle of nerves but still a sight to behold that took my breath away.

Her long red hair was sweeping down her back in loose curls, and she gave her makeup a lighter touch, resembling the girl I'd fallen in love with.

But what caused a stirring in my pants was that she'd worn a modest sundress. It wasn't like the sexy, slinky dress she'd worn that first night, and yet there was something about the simple calico cotton hugging her curves in all the right places that had my imagination racing.

I wanted to take her back to the lake, lift that skirt up over her hips, and slide into her, making her scream out in pleasure.

At my perusal, her eyes widened. "Is this okay? Should I change?" She nervously clutched the bakery box in her hands.

"No, Bella. You're gorgeous as always. Just a little too gorgeous for my libido. We might have to make a stop before we get to my house."

She looked at me sideways. "Oh, no, I remember how important it was for you to be on time for these dinners. There's no way I'm going to be the reason you're late," she said, shifting her skirt around her knees as I closed the door after her.

When I got in the truck, the smell of whatever was in that bakery box had taken over the cab. I inhaled deeply. "That smells delicious … is that what I think it is?"

She smiled. "Yeah, I remembered how much she likes them. I don't know if she still does, but I thought I'd take a chance."

I gave her a warm smile as I cranked the engine, remembering the first time Emma met my mother and presented her with a slice of cake from the bakery at the resort. It was triple chocolate with chocolate mousse and chocolate shavings on top. My mother had taken one bite of that chocolate treat before her eyes rolled up in her head. She'd said it was the best cake she'd ever tasted. And there had been many times over the years when Maria had been asked to order the cake special for Mom's birthday. Thankfully, my mom had been kind enough not to ask me to go anywhere near Pine Crest after everything that went down with Emma and her family.

The smell brought back memories, but right then, I only focused on the sweet ones.

As we drove to my childhood home, I coached Emma, "Things may get tense tonight if Silvia shows up. She and

Mama have not been on speaking terms in quite some time."

"And if Silvia doesn't show up?" Emma inquired.

I let out a long sigh. "I don't know. They may not make amends before my mom dies. I've tried everything I can think of to get through to Silvia, but she's stubborn. Ironically, she's just like Mama, which makes it even more difficult to deal with. I don't want her to find out the hard way that life is short, and we only get so much time before it's gone," I replied before I thought better of it. But then I noticed Emma was quiet, and I looked over and saw her staring out the window, worry creasing her brow.

"Oh, hey, I'm sorry. What am I doing? If this is making you think about—"

She turned to me and gave me a watery smile. "Jaime, you don't have to edit your thoughts because it might remind me of my mother. To tell you the truth, there's very little that doesn't remind me of my mother. But that's okay because they're lovely memories. I was just thinking I really hope Silvia shows up. Those last months with my mom were precious, and I rely on those memories a lot to get me through. I don't know what I'd do if I didn't have them."

I wanted to pull the truck over and wrap her in my arms to erase the sad look from her face. Instead, I stared out the windshield, thinking about my mother and hoping tonight went well.

Maybe after dinner was over, Emma and I could talk about what was bothering her, but for now, I needed to help bring my family together before it was too late.

There was no sign of Silvia's car as we pulled up to my house, and I couldn't help the stab of disappointment. Even though I knew her absence would mean less drama, I really wanted her to be there.

I walked up the steps to the front door and kept my arm slung around Emma's waist. I could hear her sucking in a nervous breath before I opened the door, but as soon as we crossed the threshold, she was all smiles. Emma could talk to anybody, and there wasn't a challenge she wouldn't face head-on.

Still, I felt for her. Facing down Esmeralda Acosta was no easy task even when you were related to her, and considering Emma was the girl who broke her baby boy's heart? I'd be nervous, too.

The first face to appear was a glowing Maria. "Emma?" she asked, beaming. "Is that you?" she continued, putting her arms out for a hug.

I hadn't told anybody Emma was coming. I just said I was bringing a "friend."

Maria had been suspicious, but she hadn't said anything, knowing things were a little tenuous with my situation.

"Oh, my God, Maria, you're all grown up," Emma said, throwing her arms around her.

"And out," Maria laughed as she pulled back, showing off her impressive belly.

Emma grinned at her. "Jaime told me he'd be an uncle soon. Congratulations! Although it's a little hard for me to wrap my brain around you being a mom. Seems like just yesterday you were still in pigtails."

"Yeah, sometimes it's hard for me to wrap my brain around, too. Then I have days where all I can feel is her kicking to get out, and there's no doubt it's real," Maria said, laughing. "It's so good to see you again," she said, putting her arm around Emma's shoulder and walking her to the dining room. "I can't wait to hear about everything you've been up to."

Their voices faded as my little sister stole the woman I loved away, but my heart warmed at the sight of them. The house was full of the smell of Sunday dinner, and I was immediately comforted. No matter how much our circumstances were changing, especially with Mama, some things remained the same.

When Maria launched herself at Emma, I'd swiped the cake from Emma's hands to save it, and now, I carried it to the kitchen. I wasn't expecting to find my mother there looking pensive.

"Mama?" I asked, concerned.

She eyed me, worry etched on her face. "Jaime, that girl you just brought into the house … have I met her?"

She was genuinely curious, not accusatory.

"Yes, Mama. A long time ago," I replied.

"She broke your heart," she said matter-of-factly.

I sucked in a long breath. "Well, yes, I guess you could say she did. But we were kids, and she didn't mean to." I found in situations like that, it was easiest to explain things simply to Mama instead of bogging her down with all the details.

She watched me for a moment, and she didn't look like my mother, but a young, scared girl. "I don't remember her—how could I forget the person who broke my baby's heart? Jaime, what is happening to me?"

I could see the tears in her eyes, and I rushed to her, putting my arms around her. "Mama, it's okay. Please don't cry. Sometimes when we get older, we get forgetful. But don't worry, we're here to help you remember, okay? You're in a house full of people who love you. We won't let you forget."

She pulled back, looking at me, tears streaming down her cheeks. "Oh, my handsome boy, you're too sweet for words, just like your father."

I swallowed hard around the lump in my throat. When Mama got her diagnosis, we were warned about how hard it would be, but nothing could prepare us for these moments. I was struggling for the right words to say when the sound of the front door opening had us turning curiously.

Silvia walked in cautiously, stopping to take in a long breath. "Well, look who the cat dragged in," my mother said, moving away from me and toward my sister. Silvia immediately tensed at the sound of our mother's voice.

"Hi, Mama," Silvia said.

"Hi, Mama? That's all you have to say to me? I don't see you for weeks at a time, and all I get is 'Hi, Mama'?" she groused.

Silvia opened her mouth to respond, but Mama just put up a hand, "Come on, you're going to make us late for dinner," and with that, she shuffled toward the dining room, leaving a startled Silvia to stand gaping at me.

I shrugged. "You heard the woman. Let's eat," I said, trying to sound jovial as I put an arm around my sister's shoulder, hoping she could derive some comfort from the gesture. "I'm really glad you're here," I whispered in her ear as we made our way to the dining room.

She made a face. "Jury's still out for me." As soon as we hit the doorway, Silvia stopped and exclaimed in surprise, "Emma?"

Emma smiled from her seat next to Maria and rose to greet Silvia as Silvia rushed around the table and gave her a big hug. "My God, I can't believe you're actually here. I heard you were back in town, but I never expected to see you *here*." I was glad Silvia seemed so relieved by Emma's presence. Maybe that would help dinner go a little more smoothly.

Before Silvia could start picking Emma's brain, Mama took her place at the head of the table and announced, "There will be time for chitchat in a minute, but first we say grace."

We took our seats obediently and joined hands. I couldn't help but squeeze Emma's hand as Mama said grace. As she smiled warmly at me, my mind imagined a lifetime of Sunday family dinners with this woman by my side.

Slow down, Jaime.

My heart definitely knew what it wanted, but I would be a fool to think everything would just magically fall into place. Emma had been through a lot and had some big decisions to make before I had any hope of keeping her around permanently. I had to be patient.

The conversation was formal at first. We kept to safe topics like how things were going at work or Maria's impending bundle of joy. Soon, Mama started talking about the joys of having a daughter, and Silvia's disgruntled sighs were audible.

"Is there something you wish to add, Silvia?" Mama asked tersely, and the food I'd been chewing turned to sawdust in my mouth. Maria and Emma stilled, watching carefully even as they continued to push their food around.

For a split second, I saw the same expression on Silvia's face as I had when we were children and she'd gotten in trouble, but it was quickly replaced with obstinance. Sucking in a deep breath, she forged ahead, "Well, Mother, I just find it ironic you preach the closeness of the mother/daughter relationship when you threw out your eldest daughter over your own prejudice."

Maria let out a long sigh, muttering, "Jesus, Mary, and Joseph," and Emma's hand squeezed my thigh beneath the table though I wasn't sure if that was meant to comfort me or reassure herself. "Silvia," I started, feeling like I needed to say something as the oldest, but Mama wasn't having it.

"No, Jaime. It's okay. I can fight my own battles though I am confused why Silvia is picking a fight. I would never throw out one of my children …"

Silvia snickered. "Maybe not literally, but your attitude told me everything I needed to know. I opened myself up to you, brought someone I cared about to meet you, and you spent the whole time making your disapproval known."

"How?" my mother demanded to know.

"Maybe this isn't the time or place—" Maria started, but Mama put up her hand to shush her, and Maria obeyed.

"Are you kidding me? You kept saying things like 'you brought *her* here' and 'this *woman* is who you are with?' I mean, it doesn't get more transparent than that. I was terrified to come out to you, and it turns out all my fears were justified."

Our mother sprang from her seat, nearly knocking the chair over in the process, and everyone tensed even further. "How dare you come into this house—my house—and show me such disrespect? It's one thing to put up with your sulky attitude, Silvia, but I will not have you coming in here and implying I'm a bigot. Especially not toward my own daughter."

Silvia stared at our mother sullenly, and my hand found Emma's beneath the table, and that time, I knew for sure I was holding onto it for my comfort. Emma cut her eyes to me and gave me a reassuring smile.

My mother continued, "Why on earth didn't you tell me this was how you felt? I would have been more than happy to explain."

"Explain what, Mama? That you didn't want a lesbian for a daughter? Maybe I wasn't ready to hear you say the words," Silvia said, and even though she sounded tough, tears welled up in her eyes.

"Silvia," our mother breathed in shock as she sank back into her chair. "I've always wanted you, mija, no matter who you love, as long as they make you happy. Don't you know that?" she asked, her voice cracking. "My memory may be fading, but I remember that day perfectly. Nothing I said had anything to do with you preferring to date women and everything to do with the *woman* you brought to my house."

Silvia's brow furrowed. "What?"

Mama let out an exasperated sigh. "You kept going on and on about this woman, but I could tell you weren't happy. You were changing all these things about yourself just to make her happy. Then when I finally got to meet her, she showed up late for dinner, complained about the food, and talked over people. My little girl deserves someone who treats her like the queen she is, and that trash was not worth your time!"

Mama's pronouncement was followed by a long, strained silence until Maria offered, "Um Silvia, not to pile on, but that girl was totally trash."

I couldn't help it. The tone of Maria's voice made me choke back a laugh, and before I knew it, everyone at the table was laughing, including Mama and Silvia.

Once we caught our breaths, Maria muttered, "I cannot believe all this was a simple misunderstanding. Emma, you must think we're nuts."

Emma smiled as all eyes turned to her. "No, not at all. It's not like my family doesn't have its fair share of crazy."

Mama observed Emma, then spoke. "Emma with the emerald eyes."

Emma's eyes widened, but Mama continued, "I remember you now. Jaime would come home with stars in his eyes, talking about his 'Emma with the emerald eyes.'"

Emma's gaze shot to mine, and I could feel my face burning. It didn't help that Maria and Silvia were chiming in with, "Oooh, Emma with emerald eyes, oooh, my fair Emma."

Mama's expression turned stern. "You two quit teasing your brother. Emma, tell me," she said, facing Emma now, and the fingers that had been grasping my thigh were now digging into me. "Is your father as bullheaded and unreasonable as he was before?"

"Mama," Maria hissed, but Emma was more than gracious.

She smiled slowly, and I could tell she was trying to come up with a diplomatic answer, but after a moment, she let out a long breath before laughing and admitting, "To be honest, ma'am, yes, he is."

Her answer surprised me. She was always so careful about how she talked about her family, but that was probably the most honest thing I'd ever heard her say regarding her father.

Mama nodded in approval at her honest response. "I see. I can't say I'm too surprised. Some old goats refuse to evolve. As long as he's not still pulling your strings, you'll be good enough for my boy."

"Mom," I threatened.

Mama looked at me with wide eyes. "What? The Emma I remember was not a stupid girl. She knows I'm speaking the truth."

I opened my mouth to speak, but Emma cut in, "She's right, Jaime. I messed up back then. He was pulling all the strings, but," she continued, straightening in her chair, "I'm my own woman now, making my own choices."

"Amen to that. Who needs a man making choices for you?" Silvia said, raising her glass.

Mama and Maria laughed, raising their glasses as well, and I laughed in delight to see Emma being embraced by my family even as I wondered if what she said was true. Was she really no longer controlled by her father's wishes? If so, then we might actually have a shot at making this work.

God, please …

After dinner, Emma was hugged within an inch of her life by the women in my family and told to come back soon.

It warmed my heart, especially knowing my mother's reservations, but Emma was so charming; none of them stood a chance against her. I was also relieved Silvia and my mother reconciled. It had been a good evening—one I didn't want to end just yet.

After Emma and I climbed into my truck to head back to her hotel, I asked, "Are you up for a detour, Miss Carter?"

She smiled, and even in the dark of the truck cab, I could see the excitement in her eyes. "I'm always up for a detour with you."

Giddiness raced up my spine as we went in the opposite direction of the resort, reaching the outskirts of town. As we approached our destination, Emma's eyes lit up when she recognized where we were. I turned off the main road onto a dark driveway that wove through the trees until we hit a clearing and found the remnants of an old drive-in theater where we used to come as kids.

When I put the truck in park and turned off the engine, I looked over to find her biting her lip excitedly.

"I've been waiting to kiss you all night," I told her, leaning toward her across the bench seat as she lunged at me, our mouths meeting enthusiastically.

The fantasy she'd revealed earlier had been burning in my brain ever since. I would do anything to fulfill her fantasies, and thankfully, this one was pretty easy to accomplish.

She broke away from my mouth long enough to say, "I can't believe this is finally happening," before her mouth started trailing kisses down my neck as her fingers started fiercely working at the buttons on my shirt.

I chuckled at her eagerness, but when she undid the snap of my jeans, the laugh died in my throat.

"Bella," I whispered, hearing the strain in my voice, needing to taste her again like I needed air.

Our mouths fused together as our hands wandered all over each other like lovesick teenagers, and that was exactly how I felt.

Even though we'd spent the last several nights exploring one another, there was something about being in the cab of the truck, reliving those moments when we almost took it too far. But now there was no going back—I wanted her in every way.

When my tongue delved into her mouth to taste her again, her hand dove into my pants beneath the waistband of my boxers, and her delicate fingers wrapped around my shaft, stroking me as I groaned into our kiss. "God, you're amazing. Your hands feel so good on my cock. Do you like stroking me like that?"

I could feel her smile against my lips. "I do. But I think I'd like it even better with you in my mouth."

And that was when, to my surprise, she shoved me back into my seat and dropped to the floor of the truck so she was on her hands and knees with her head over my lap. She locked eyes with me as her hands stroked my cock, and I let out a moan of appreciation not just of her touch but in anticipation of what she was about to do.

I should've been embarrassed to admit there hadn't been a whole lot of foreplay the few times Emma and I had been together. We'd just needed to be as close to each other as quickly as possible.

"Bella," I growled in a ragged breath. Her smile grew before her hair fell over her face, and she leaned down, jerking my shaft free of my underwear and flicking her tongue against my tip.

I hissed in agony and pleasure, trying to keep my hips from bucking up toward her mouth. I could feel her husky laugh against the sensitive skin, and then her tongue was swirling around the head of my dick. Before I could draw in a breath, she sucked down half my shaft, eagerly moaning in the back of her throat. Just that sound alone was enough to make me completely unravel, and I was loving every goddamn second of it.

As she took me into her hot, wet mouth inch by inch, I gritted my teeth against the incredible sensation. That was my Emma, on her hands and knees, giving me the fantasy of a lifetime and groaning in pleasure because of it.

I swept her hair away from her face and gently fisted my hands in her hair so I could watch her slowly glide up and down my hard shaft.

I felt like if I took a breath, everything would shatter into a million pieces, and I didn't want this feeling of closeness to stop.

She'd shown vulnerability earlier that night at dinner when discussing her father and her vehement conviction she was her own woman now. And now she was being vulnerable with me in another way. All the pain of the last twelve years seemed to melt away beneath her ministrations.

As much as I wanted this to go on forever, I also desperately needed to be inside her. I needed to look her in the eyes as I took her in the cab of that truck. "Emma, my love, please, I need to be inside you," I begged, "I need to feel your tight pussy around me," and with that, I helped her into a sitting position, sliding her panties down and yanking the skirt of her dress up over her waist. I kissed her fiercely as my hands explored her folds, thrilled to find them soaked. She was ready for me.

I laid her on the bench seat, peppering kisses over her face. She moaned against my mouth, "Jaime, that was so hot. I loved feeling your hard cock in my mouth," she said, and I groaned.

"Well, I hope you love the feeling of me sliding inside you just as much."

"I do. I love all of you," she said as her hand reached to position me at her opening.

All the emotions I'd been trying to keep in check for so long were no match for that confession. Everything in me broke apart, and I surged inside her as she cried out. I buried my face into her neck. "Fuck, Emma, I love you so much," I said, thrusting into her. "I always have." I said the words, and I fucking meant them because there in the dark cab of my truck as I fulfilled her fantasy, there was no stopping the truth pouring from my lips. She was the woman I loved, the only woman I'd ever loved, and I wanted her to know it.

Her hips struggled to keep up with mine as I pounded into her, swallowing her cries with my mouth and tasting her as her pussy began to spasm around my shaft.

She ran her nails down my back as my thrusts became more frantic. The sound of her pants, moans, and screams would be branded as a soundtrack on my brain.

"That's my good girl. Come for me," I coaxed as I felt her tightening around me, desperate to hold back my release until she was fully satisfied.

Her hands shot to my ass, digging her fingers into my skin as she pulled me deeper and cried out my name, the syllables filling the cab of that truck reverberating through my hypersensitized body. She came hard around me, and I followed almost immediately, shouting out my release.

I collapsed on top of her, trying to catch my breath and loving the fact that every time I inhaled, I was surrounded by the scent of the woman I loved. I felt almost feral, gathering her up in my arms and holding her close to me, whispering nonsensical, sweet nothings into her ear.

When I finally regained my senses, I realized what I was saying. "I never want to let you go. Don't make me let you go. I can't do it again."

Startled I'd let myself go so completely, I pulled back and looked at her face to see her eyes shining with tears, but she was smiling at me.

She reached for my face, rubbing her thumbs over my cheeks, admitting, "I don't want to let you go either … I won't let anyone get in our way ever again."

Relief flooded my body as I leaned down to kiss her, and soon, we were feverishly making out again.

I would have stayed with her all night, holding her, and making plans for the future except for the insistent ringing of my phone.

I ignored it the first two times, but then Emma said, "Maybe you should answer that. What if it's Maria or Silvia?"

I dug my phone out of my pocket and answered. "Jaime," Maria's voice sounding strained, "I need your help. Mama doesn't recognize me, and she's freaking out, trying to lock me out of the house."

"Shit, hang in there. I'll be there as soon as I can."

I hung up the phone and glanced at Emma, concern etched on her face. "Mama doesn't recognize Maria," I explained while I quickly rearranged my clothing and fired up the engine.

She stayed in the center seat next to me instead moving over to the passenger side and rubbed my arm as I rushed back to the resort. "I hate you have to go through this with your mother, Jaime, but she's lucky to have kids who are so patient and determined to stick by her side."

I laughed. "That's how we were raised. No one gets left behind."

Emma's touch stiffened slightly, and I grimaced internally. Before I could clarify, she said, "That's a good quality to have."

We pulled up to the front of the resort, and I was about to open my door and walk her to her room, but she stopped me. "Jaime, that sounded pretty urgent. I can get myself to my room though I appreciate your chivalry."

"Are you sure?" I inquired, and she huffed out a laugh, kissing me sweetly. "Jaime, I can manage, but call me any hour of the night if you need to talk," she said, kissing me again, more deeply that time. I wanted nothing more than to follow her back to her room, but she was right. I needed to get home to Mama.

"Goodnight, Bella," I whispered against her lips.

"Goodnight, Jaime. Sweet dreams."

I didn't pull away from the curb until I saw her disappear behind the double doors of the resort. I thanked my lucky stars that brilliant woman understood how important my family was to me.

I rushed home uncertain of what I was waiting for me, but it couldn't dampen the warmth in my chest when I thought about the time we spent in each other arms.

Emma

Even though I missed Jaime's touch, I knew he needed to get home, and I prayed Jaime and Maria could calm Mama Acosta swiftly. I couldn't imagine how difficult it must be to watch someone you love gradually disappearing before your eyes.

I was lost in thought, reliving our time in the truck and his words said in the heat of the moment …

Except they weren't in the heat of the moment. Jaime doesn't say things he doesn't mean.

That reminder made me smile wider even as it twisted at my heart. Jaime was never one to mince words, so when in the heat of passion, he announced he loved me and always had, I knew in my heart he was speaking his truth just as I had when I'd told him I loved him, too.

Now that the truth was out there, I needed to face my father—and I wouldn't let him take Jaime away from me a second time.

I let out a sigh as I ambled down the hall toward the elevator. First thing tomorrow, I would send an SOS text to Caroline and Sophie for an emergency meeting. They'd offered to help me figure out this thing with my father, and I was finally going to take them up on it. Not that I couldn't figure it out for myself, but I was eager to move on with my life with the man I loved, and at that moment, I couldn't believe I'd put it off for so long. It was now or never.

But for tonight, I wouldn't dwell on my father and allow him to dampen the afterglow of my evening. It had been a beautiful night, and I would relish every moment.

I'd just pushed the button for the elevator when I heard a slurred voice behind me say, "Well, well, well, look who decided to spend the night in her own room."

I turned to see an obviously drunk Andrew.

"Andrew? Are you okay?"

He ignored my question. "You know, I heard rumblings you were running around with the bartender, but it's a sight to behold to see you stumbling out of that dirty old truck—you look like you had a good time tonight, Emma."

"Andrew, you've obviously had too much to drink. Why don't you go back to your room and sleep it off?"

"No, not until you tell me why?"

"Why what?"

"Why you picked him over me? I know I look like a buttoned-up guy, but I could be just as wild as him. Is that what turns you on? The Latino heat? Why don't you come over here, and I'll show you what kind of heat I can give you," he said, lurching toward me.

I looked around frantically. It was late and most of the guests were in their rooms. The elevator door opened, and I worried he would shove me inside. He was bigger than me and could easily overpower me.

"I'm not choosing him over you. We work together—you were never an option," I tried to explain as calmly as possible.

"Bullshit, you can't tell me you didn't feel that thing between us. Even our fathers knew we would hit it off, and they were right … you're the one who's causing a problem. But I'm a fixer, and I'm going to fix this problem," he said, leaning down.

I tried to move away from him, but I was cornered. Just when I thought he would make contact, Andrew suddenly fell to his knees.

I looked up in shock to see Charlie, a bartender at the hotel, with one hand grasping the back of Andrew's neck and the other restraining his arm behind his back. Charlie was a decent-sized man but not as tall as Andrew, and yet he'd forced him to his knees with ease.

"I believe the lady said no, jackass," Charlie said through gritted teeth.

"Hey, you need to mind your own business," Andrew dared, throwing a glare over his shoulder, but when he caught the look on Charlie's face—a stony mask of fury—he stuttered, then shut up.

"Now, I think you should follow her suggestion and sleep it off. Otherwise, I'll be forced to finish the job."

Andrew didn't say anything for a long moment before staggering to his feet and stumbling into the elevator. Muttering under his breath as the doors closed, he scowled at both Charlie and me.

As soon as the doors shut, Charlie turned to me. "Are you okay?"

"Yeah," I said, shuddering. "I have no idea what that was about."

"I'll call security, and we'll get him out of here," Charlie said, turning away.

"No," I said, putting out a hand to stop him. "That won't be necessary. He's just had too much to drink. I'm sure he'll be regretful in the morning."

Charlie looked doubtful, then said, "Fine, but I'm going to walk you back to your room."

"That's not necessary … " I started, but Charlie cut me off.

"Jaime would never forgive me if I let you go up there by yourself, so I'm walking you to your room and making sure you're locked in for the night. And I put the staff on alert to not serve that guy."

I nodded, "Okay. Thank you."

Charlie and I rode up in the elevator to the top floor in silence. I knew he had questions but bit his tongue.

Once he'd delivered me safely to my room, I locked the door behind me and sagged against it, letting out a long breath.

What the hell was that?

I wasn't sure, but I knew my "working relationship" with Andrew Jr. was officially over. Even if he was too sauced to realize what he was doing or the consequences, I wasn't comfortable anymore.

Despite the late hour, I pulled out my phone and, with shaking hands, dialed my father.

He answered groggily, "Emma, why are you calling at this hour?"

I let out a long breath, "I'm sorry, Dad, but this couldn't wait. We've run into a problem with the Travers'."

That had his attention, and I could hear him sober almost instantly. "What's going on? What happened?"

"Dad, I've tried to be patient with Andrew, but he keeps stalling and making unwanted advances, and tonight, when I returned to the hotel, he tried to force himself on me."

"Force himself? How?"

Embarrassed, I relayed the incident in the hotel lobby. My dad was silent for a long moment.

This was the part where I expected him to blow up on my behalf and call the whole thing off.

I didn't expect his next words. "Dammit, Emma. This should've been a slam dunk," he fumed. I was stunned to silence, but he wasn't done. "I thought you were mature enough to handle going back home, but I should've known the minute you got near that boy it would be trouble. It's obvious you can't handle the basic task I've assigned you, so I'm going to have to clean up this mess myself."

I finally got my lips to work as I asked in sheer confusion, "I don't get it, Dad. You've never tolerated that kind of behavior from a client before, especially toward me. I'm shocked you're reacting this way."

"Grow up, Emma. You can't hide behind your mother's skirt forever. You're playing with the big dogs now, and your feelings are going to get stomped on. You can't afford to be too sensitive. Besides, there's no way I'm killing this deal. The stakes are just too damn high."

"But, Dad …"

He cut me off. "Is this the only reason you called so late at night? I should've guessed. Listen to me, I want you to put your game face on because, tomorrow, you're going to salvage what you can of this deal, and I'll see what I can do with the old man from here. Goodnight," he sneered and hung up before I could answer.

For the second time in not so many days, I had the urge to throw my phone across the room. But this was a different kind of anger. My heart was breaking as I realized I'd lost my father. He was no longer in my corner, protecting me and wanting the best for me.

So I did something I probably shouldn't have—I didn't tell anybody what happened. I didn't phone Caroline to rant. I didn't talk to Jaime and admit I was in over my head. I didn't even make the effort the following morning to go for a hike to clear my head and talk to my mom.

Something in me shut down after the call with my father. I knew I should at least talk to Caroline and Sophie, but I wasn't ready to say the words out loud because then it would be true. My father had betrayed me, and he'd betrayed the memory of my mother.

I just wasn't ready to accept it.

So I locked myself away and fixated on it, shutting myself off from those who could help me.

Jaime

♥

I should've called Emma after everything settled down with my mother, but by the time I finally got Mama to sleep, it was so late I didn't want to wake her. So I just sent her a quick text goodnight and fell into an exhausted stupor.

Despite the difficult ending to the night, when I woke the next morning, my mom seemed to be in better spirits, and I let my mind wander to the evening I'd shared the night before with the woman I loved.

But as soon as I walked into work, I was greeted by a very concerned Charlie.

"Do I want to know? Did Ashley show up late again? Or did Joey forget to prep the fruit?"

Charlie just looked at me and then nodded to my office behind the bar. Once inside, he closed the door behind him, and a knot of worry formed at the bottom of my stomach.

"Listen, man, you know I'm not anybody's keeper, and I definitely don't like to stick my nose where it doesn't belong, but something kept me up all night, and I feel you need to know."

"Okay," I said, drawing out the two syllables. "Don't leave me in suspense. What's up?"

He relayed what happened in the lobby with Emma and her business associate, Andrew.

"You've got to be fucking kidding me." I growled.

"No, I'm not. I couldn't decide whether I was going to tell you, but when you came in whistling, I figured you must not know. I wanted to throw the guy out, but she insisted he just needed to sleep it off. Kinda blew my mind he'd lay a hand on her like that. This is not good, bro." I nodded in agreement. "I'm not sure how you want to handle it, but if you need backup, I'm here," he offered.

"Thank you, man. I appreciate it, and I'm really thankful you were here to help Emma."

He shook his head. "No problem. But you'll probably want to check on her. She said she was fine, but she looked pretty shaken up."

Before I could respond, there was a knock at the door.

I didn't want to deal with whoever it was, but reluctantly, I said, "Come in."

It was Ashley, one of the servers.

"Sorry to interrupt, but did you know there are surveyors behind the resort?"

The word surveyor made the knot of worry in my stomach grow exponentially. The Lounge bar and restaurant faced the back of the resort, and the land belonged to Emma now that her mother was gone.

It remained untouched, exactly the way her mother had wanted it. At least, that was what Emma explained to me when I asked her why she felt so loyal to the family business and Pine Crest. She needed to protect her mother's legacy, and her legacy was that land. Knowing surveyors were there made ice trickle down my spine.

"No, I hadn't heard, but I'm going to find out what's going on" I said before quickly weaving my way through the back of the bar with Charlie hot on my heels as I went out the back exit and found two men with surveying equipment.

"Excuse me, gentlemen. What are you doing?"

The two men stopped and turned, looking confused.

"We were contracted by Pine Crest Resorts to survey the land. We have permits."

"And who signed those contracts? I know the woman who owns this land, and there's no way she would hire surveyors."

One of the men produced a folded piece of paper from his work vest. I looked down at the permit, which had a bunch of legal gibberish, but it clearly stated John Carter had hired them.

"Fuck," I bit off.

"I'm guessing Emma doesn't know?" Charlie asked. He must have been reading over my shoulder.

I shook my head. "I can guarantee she has no idea," I seethed as I handed the permit back to the surveyor and turned to Charlie. "Please don't say anything about this to the staff. I need to sort this out first—and I need to talk to Emma."

"Better make that sooner rather than later," Charlie suggested, "I'll hold down the fort here while you talk to her."

I didn't need to be told twice.

I raced to the elevator, cursing every drawn-out second it took to arrive, and I only let out a breath when I got to Emma's floor. When I arrived at her door, there was a do not disturb sign hung on the handle, but that wouldn't stop me.

I knocked on the door, and when there was no answer, I called through the door, "Emma? It's Jaime. I need to see you."

I let out a sigh of relief when she answered, but my chest clenched when I saw her face and the dark rings around her eyes.

I rushed in, taking her into my arms. "Come here, baby. Are you okay?"

She gently pushed off me, shrugging off my concern. "I'm fine … but what's wrong with you? You look like you've seen a ghost. Do I look that bad?"

"You're always the most beautiful woman in the room," I responded as I followed her through the room. "I heard about last night and needed to make sure you were alright."

She had a tight smile on her lips when she turned back to me. "He just had too much to drink. It's no big deal. "

"The man put his hands on you and had you cornered. That's a big fucking deal."

She looked at me, determination in her eyes. "I appreciate your concern, Jaime, but I am a grown woman. I can take care of myself."

I hesitated before responding, realizing I might be on thin ice here. Emma was so used to taking care of everything herself it was hard for her to accept help. "I *know* you can, I just … tell me you're not going to be alone with this guy anymore, please?"

She huffed out a laugh. "I'll do my best." Her face softened when she took into my expression. "I'll be careful, Jaime. I promise. And I'm going to do everything I can to wrap this thing up because …"

"Because?"

She shook her head. "Because it's been a pain in my ass, and, frankly, it's time to move on."

I wasn't sure if she was referring to the business deal or being in Silverpine, but I didn't have time to overthink her comment.

"Well, I hate to be the bearer of bad news, but when I got to work this morning, we found surveyors assessing the land behind the resort."

Her eyebrows raised in surprise. "Seriously?"

"Yeah," I confirmed. "I confronted them, and they showed me the permit—it was authorized by your dad."

"*Fuck*," Emma cursed, something I didn't hear her do often, and then she looked at me with a strained smile. "I'm sure it's nothing. I'll talk to him about it," she said a little too casually.

"Emma, you know if there's something going on, you can talk to me about it."

"I appreciate the offer, but I've got this covered. Don't worry, Jaime."

"Emma," I pleaded. "There's obviously something going on here. I know you'd never go against your mother's wishes, so why the hell would surveyors come anywhere near this place?"

"Jaime," she sighed, "I told you. I have it covered. My dad is thorough and likes to know what's going on around the resort. That's probably all this is." I let out a sigh of frustration before I could stop myself, and she looked at me sharply. "What? Just say it—whatever it is you're thinking, just say it."

I ran a frustrated hand through my hair. "He's doing it again. "

"And by 'again,' you mean?"

"He's calling the shots, pulling the strings. He's deciding for you."

Her lips flattened into an irritated line. "I know he's done that in the past, but I am a grownup. There's no way I would let him do that again."

"Maybe not intentionally, but he's vindictive and sneaky, Emma. You know that by now."

She stood, looking irritated. "You think I don't know my own father?"

I let out a frustrated growl. "No. You probably know him better than anyone, but you also give him the most leeway, and at some point, it has to stop. He's already made some pretty life altering decision on your behalf. I'd hate to see what happens if you don't learn to stand up to him now," I said as she put up a hand to stop me, and I immediately regretted my words.

"That's enough. I am sick and tired of people telling me what I should and shouldn't do and the dire consequences that await me. I have worked really hard to get where I am, and I'm not stupid."

"Emma, you're the smartest, most talented woman I know. It's just …"

"It's just you still think of me as that naive teenager who let him drive a wedge between us?"

I bit my tongue, kicking myself for not having done it sooner.

"I get it. You still have an axe to grind with him. No one understands that more than me, Jaime. But I have my mother's legacy to protect, so that means dealing with him. Which is what I intend to do in my own way, and in my own time. I just need everyone to get off my back and let me figure out the best way to approach him. I realize his behavior makes him seem like some evil, capitalistic swine, but he's my father, and he'd never want to see me get hurt."

I couldn't stop the snicker that came out or the words that followed. "Could've fooled me."

"Excuse me?"

I was in it now, no turning back. "The man coerced you into leaving me, the man you loved. He makes you his workhorse for years on end, taking advantage of your grief over your mother's death. You jump through all his stupid hoops, and it's still not enough. Now he's letting some creep go after you? What kind of man does that?"

Fire lit in her eyes, and I knew there was no backtracking. "I think you said everything there is to say. Now, if you would please leave, I have work to do."

I let out another exasperated groan. "Emma, please, I'm just pointing out what the rest of the world sees. I'm not trying to hurt your feelings or tell you what to do."

"Well, you could've fooled me," she said with a grim smile as she parroted my words back to me. "I'll see you later, Jaime," she insisted, effectively dismissing me as she strode to the bathroom.

I waited for a moment, debating whether I should stick it out and make her talk to me, but I figured I'd be no better than her father or the schmuck from the other night if I forced her into a corner she didn't want to be in.

I had to give her space and let us cool down. In the meantime, I would figure out what the fuck her father was up to.

Emma

I waited until I heard the door to the suite close, then let the tears fall. Despite wallowing in my tumultuous emotions all night, I kept the tears at bay, holding onto my anger and fixating on all the ugly words my father had said to me.

Jaime wasn't wrong, but I didn't need to hear it again. I was still trying to wrap my head around the fact my dad didn't care about my wellbeing or honoring my mother's wishes. Deep down, I'd known all along, but the confirmation was staring me in the face, and I couldn't ignore it anymore. I felt like I was losing another parent.

I glimpsed myself in the mirror and bit back a groan at the raccoon eyes and tear-streaked redness.

I needed to get out of here and get some air. It was what I should've done first thing instead of moping around my hotel room all morning, avoiding talking to Jaime or Caroline and Sophie.

I would have to deal with the situation soon, but I needed some time to clear my head.

Nothing in haste, my love.

The words flitted through my head, clear and concise, and from a voice I hadn't heard in far too long.

"Mom?"

There was no response, but my brain replayed the words, "Nothing in haste, my love."

That was what she'd used to tell me when I was younger and torn up about making a decision. I always felt pressure to make the right decision. I'd never wanted to disappoint my father, but my mom had been a big fan of taking your time. She'd believed you could never be too late for an opportunity because you'd be just on time for the thing meant for you.

I'd been up all night worrying about how to best tell my father to fuck off without losing what I'd worked so hard for and protecting what was my mother's. But I suddenly realized I didn't need to run myself ragged trying to figure it out. It was time to take a page from Lydia Carter's book and take my time.

With that in mind, I got dressed and left the resort. I didn't look over to the bar to see Jaime watching me as I exited the lobby. I drove my rental car to Rainbow Lake, where I stored my rowing scull and oars.

It had been way too long since I'd been on the water, but soon, I was in the zone. Calm washed over me, and my mind no longer raced. The rhythmic click of the oar in the oarlock, the roll of the seat, the controlled breaths required with each stroke. I was too busy focusing on my technique to overthink the mess I found myself in.

I left everything on the water—my anger, my frustration, my sadness. As I coasted into the dock, I felt more at peace about what I needed to do.

It was time to round up the troops.

"Do you know why she called this meeting?" I heard Caroline say quietly to Sophie through the screen of the laptop.

"No, but I figure it's huge if she's doing it in the middle of the day. What exactly are we waiting for?" Sophie asked.

"We," I broke in, "are waiting for room service. Sophie, are you someplace where you can get an enormous glass of wine?"

Sophie's eyes widened. "Does cooking sherry count?"

Caroline made a face at the suggestion, but then Sophie's eyes brightened, and she said, "Oh, wait, we do have some bourbon for our Kentucky bourbon cake in the pantry. Hold on a second. I'll be right back."

Caroline looked over her shoulder at me. "Encouraging her to drink on the job, are you? You're really starting to worry me, Emma."

I settled down next to my best friend of many years. "No need to fret. Today is the day I put all of your worries to rest—with your help, of course."

"And we need to be tipsy for that?"

I shrugged, smiling. "How do we hatch our best plans? It's usually over a glass of wine or margaritas. Sue me for wanting to remain authentic."

There was a knock at the door and the call of "room service."

I hurried over to the door to greet the server with our bottle of rosé. I gave him a generous tip and thanked him before shutting the door behind me and popping the cork. When I returned to Caroline with our glasses, Sophie had settled in and poured herself a small tumbler of bourbon. "What are we drinking to, Emma?" she asked.

"We are drinking to my freedom."

"I'm intrigued, but what exactly does that mean?" Caroline asked.

"It means I finally see my father for who he is, and …" Emotions clogged my throat, and my friends rushed to comfort me as I heard Sophie say "Oh Emma" while Caroline put an arm around my shoulder, squeezing it gently.

I cleared my throat, willing myself to get through this. "It's taken me a long time to accept he's not capable of being the parent I need him to be. I've held on to hope for too long, and it's time to let it go."

My friends looked at me sympathetically. After a long pause, Caroline declared, "Well, it's about damn time. Here's to your independence," she said, clinking glasses with mine as Sophie held hers up to the screen, and we all took a drink.

"So, what's the plan now that daddy dearest is no longer calling the shots?" Sophie asked.

"Well, that's where I could use your help. I'm assuming Elizabeth has some connections to some pretty powerful attorneys?" I asked and watched Sophie's eyes widened with delight.

Sophie's mother, Elizabeth, was a political maven. She'd spent most of her life campaigning and playing the role of a "doting mother" to Sophie, all the while kicking ass and taking names to climb the ranks. Of course, her public and private personas didn't always match up, but she did the best she could with Sophie.

Sophie laughed. "Oh, yeah. The real question is, how broken do you want the old man to be in the end?"

I looked at her solemnly. "I'm going for the jugular."

"Oh, shit, Emma didn't come to play," Caroline pronounced, clapping her hands.

I filled them in on the all the details—the surveyors, the weird comments Andrew made about the land, and my father's determination to see the merger through. Then I sucked in a deep breath and told them about the night before when Andrew made his move.

"That son of a bitch," Sophie hissed.

Caroline looked at me with a furrowed brow. "Why am I just now hearing about this, and how is that man still walking around with his head on?"

"Because I played it off like it wasn't a big deal, but then Jaime confronted me about it, and we got into a big fight."

"Wait a minute, back up," Sophie said, "Jaime confronted you about this as in he was holding you responsible?"

I was quick to defend Jaime. "Oh, God, no. As soon as he found out, he came to my room to make sure I was okay and encouraged me to not to see him again or at the very least not be alone with him."

"That's reasonable," Caroline chimed in.

"It is, but I didn't take it well. I couldn't sleep last night after the incident with Andrew, and when I called my dad to tell him what happened, things got ugly. After that conversation, I knew I couldn't make excuses for him anymore but wasn't quite ready to face it. Then Jaime reminded me of all the horrible things my dad had done.

I got overwhelmed and snapped at him. Told him I could take care of myself, and I didn't need his help."

My friends looked at me warmly, but Caroline spoke first, and her words surprised me, considering how intensely independent Caroline was. "Everybody needs help, Emma. You are fiercely capable, and everyone who knows you knows that, but you don't have to shoulder everything yourself. That's what friends are for—and well-meaning boy toys," she said, referring to Jaime.

"He's not a boy toy …" I whispered.

"And the plot thickens," Sophie teased.

I shook my head. "I should've known I wouldn't be able to keep it casual with him, you know?"

"No, I couldn't possibly know. Please explain it to me like I'm five," Sophie insisted with a smile.

"I love him … I think, maybe I've always loved him?"

"Tell us something we don't know," Caroline groused.

"I guess I always felt that deep down. I just never imagined he would feel the same way."

"And you know for sure he loves you, too?" Sophie asked with eyebrows raised before adding quickly, "He'd be an idiot not to. What I mean is, has he said it?"

I could feel myself blush.

"That's a yes," Caroline stated.

"I just don't want to imagine life without him again. I was feeling like I'd have to choose between carrying on the family legacy or Jaime. It should be a no-brainer, but since my mom's gone, I feel responsible for carrying on what she started."

"Emma," Sophie murmured, "You carry on her legacy every day just by being your amazing self. I know your mom loved the resort, and she loved that land, but she loved you more."

Tears fell from my eyes as I smiled at Sophie and squeezed Caroline's hand. "I don't know what I would do without you two."

"I don't either," Caroline said, pulling me into her arms and giving me a big hug. "Here, that's from Sophie, too."

"Yes, it is," Sophie agreed. "And I hope you work things out with Jaime. I know you had a fight, but—"

"But he seems pretty great for you," Caroline added.

"I haven't even gotten to meet the guy," Sophie said. "But Caroline filled me in, and if she approves, I know he's good for you."

I looked over at Caroline, shocked. She shrugged nonchalantly. "What? I know what's good for my friends. I may not be able pick out a decent guy for myself, but for you two, it's easy." She laughed.

"You'll meet your guy soon, Caroline. I have a good feeling," Sophie announced. "And I think I know the right attorney for the job. Do you really think it will come to that?"

I shook my head, unsure. "This trip has been full of surprises, so I want to be prepared for anything my father may throw at me. I may have to give up the resort and my stake in the company, but my mom left that land to me, and I'll do anything to protect it. So far, he's been unmoved by my pleas, and I've realized if he's going to play nasty, then I need to fight fire with fire."

Sophie grinned. "I'll make the call."

Jaime

♥

Two days. It had been two days since my fight with Emma, and I was going out of my mind.

I understood she needed space, and I knew she was safe because most my staff would report to me unprompted, but I was miserable. I knew I should go to her and apologize, but I wasn't sure if she was ready to hear it. That she'd stayed away this long made me think she was still really mad.

I saw her rushing out of the hotel regularly, a woman on a mission. But she never looked over at the bar—or me.

I stood idly wiping down the bar, staring off into space, when a familiar female voice sounded in my ear. "Okay, the sister brigade has banded, and I've been sent to find out what the hell is going on with you, Jaime." I turned to see Silvia.

I quirked a brow. "I'm sorry. 'Sister brigade'?"

She shrugged. "Or sister squad, if you prefer alliteration. Makes no difference to me. All I know is Maria called me, saying you've been acting all mopey for the last couple of days. From the way she described it, I totally recognized it as woman troubles. So, what's going on between you and the fair Emma?"

I rolled my eyes and shook my head, fully prepared to make something up to get her to drop the subject, but when I opened my mouth, I told her the truth. First, I told her about the run-in Emma had with that jackass Andrew. Then I told her how I reacted and screwed it up and now Emma needed space.

Silvia listened patiently, waiting until I was finished to say, "Yeah, you definitely screwed the pooch on that one, big brother. But I don't think it's a lost cause. I mean, the worst thing she can accuse you of is being overly concerned, and Emma seems reasonable enough to understand that."

"I know. That's what I keep telling myself, but she was livid, and I can't say I blame her. Especially because her father has spent most of her life second-guessing and overriding her decisions, and then there I was doing the same thing."

"That's true, but at least you're mature enough to understand what you were doing and feel bad about it. That's more than I can say about most men, her father included. Look, if it's really bothering you this much, you need to gather up your cojones and talk to her. I know you're trying to give her space, but if you're feeling this miserable, chances are she is, too."

"Maybe," I grumped as one of my servers rushed toward me and nearly slammed her tray on the bar.

"I need two more Blanton's, Jaime."

"Sure, is everything okay out there, Ashley?"

She let out a huff. "Yeah, I'm fine. Just a couple assholes at table twelve."

I went on high alert. Unfortunately, we had a lot of wealthy clientele who thought it was acceptable to belittle the staff, but I wouldn't stand for it. I didn't let anybody mistreat our waitstaff, especially the women. "Do I need to kick them out?"

Ashley smiled at me sadly. "I wish you could … Too bad it's the owner of Pine Crest and that douchebag who's been hanging around Emma."

That had me standing at attention and Silvia sitting up straighter on her barstool.

"Mr. Carter's here? How did I not see him?"

"Because they snuck in quietly and took the corner table out of your eyesight. A little sketchy if you ask me. And I know you've been trying to rein in the rumor mill, but you're not going to like what they're talking about."

"Well?" Silvia prompted, "Lay it on us."

Ashley looked discreetly over her shoulder, then leaned in close. "They're talking about building an addition to the resort using the nature preserve out back. And don't get me started on what they're saying about Emma."

I felt my anger rise, but I had to hear it with my own ears. I nodded at Ashley, urging her to continue. "They're talking about Emma like she's human chattel. Her father is assuring this guy he'll convince her marrying him is good for everybody. That she'll fall into line as she always does."

"That motherfucker," I said under my breath, unable to stop myself.

"I second that," Silvia said. "We gotta shut this guy down."

Ashley continued. "Well, if you come up with a plan, I want in. I can't believe Mr. Carter would do this to her. It's hard to believe they're even related. I mean, I don't know her personally, but I've heard nothing but good things about her. She seems like a good person, and supposedly, her mother was an angel."

"She was, and Emma is, too," I confirmed.

"Even if she wasn't," Silvia said, "No one should talk about someone like that, much less their own child."

Ashley grabbed the tray with their drinks. "I better get back before they pitch a fit."

"Ashley," I called before she could move away, "I don't care who's at that table. If you're uncomfortable in any way, you come get me, okay?"

"Got it, boss. Thanks," she said with a smile before walking away.

"Okay, Jaime," Silvia said. "I know you're giving her some space, but this changes a lot. We've got to move fast."

"I agree. Question is, what are we going to do?"

Raising a conspiratorial brow, she said, "I think I know someone who can help us. Just give me a minute." She grabbed her phone from her purse and jumped off the barstool before shuffling somewhere more private as I wrestled with my anger and fought the urge to march over to that table and deck Mr. Carter and Andrew just for breathing.

Thankfully, Silvia wasn't gone long. And when she came back, she looked like the cat that ate the canary, grinning at me broadly and announcing, "You owe me big time, big brother. Help is on the way."

"Sounds great, but you want to fill me in on this plan you seem to have come up with without me?"

"Nothing too complicated," Silvia said, slipping back onto the stool. "I find simple is best. If she's having a hard time believing her father is really a bad dude, then we need to get undeniable proof. We have the perfect opportunity right here—they're holed up in that corner, and Ashley is plying them with liquor. Now we just need somebody sexy and charming to get them to talk ..." she said before adding, "... while we record it."

"And who do you have in mind for this endeavor? I don't feel comfortable asking anybody to offer themselves up for this kind of gig."

She smiled even wider. "Normally, I would agree, but some people are born to perform and would go out of their way for the chance to practice their craft. I happen to know a fine actress who regularly stars in productions at the community Playhouse … and she's sexy as hell."

My eyebrow shot up, and Silvia quickly continued. "She's my new girlfriend. I've been waiting to introduce her to everybody, but she's pretty amazing," she said, blushing.

I couldn't help but smile at my sister. "Are you sure she's up for this?"

Before she could answer, a tall, curvaceous brunette in a tight red dress sashayed into the bar. When the woman's eyes met my sister's, the attraction was undeniable. I felt like I was watching a cartoon where the characters got heart eyes when they saw one another.

She walked up to the bar, and Silvia slipped an arm around her waist. "Jaime, this is Jen, my girlfriend—and our last-minute savior."

Jen stuck her hand out to shake mine. "It's so good to finally meet you, Jaime. And I'm excited to be part of this scheme. I've taken down a lot of fictional dirtbags on stage, but now I get to do it in real life. It's going to be a thrill."

"I can't thank you enough for agreeing to be a part of this. It's all happening so fast."

Silvia shot me a look. "They're talking about your girl like she's an object to be sold off, Jaime. We can't make this happen fast enough." She turned to her girlfriend. "Do you have everything set up on your phone to record?"

Jen nodded. "I double-checked everything on the way over here. It's this app I use when I'm running my lines for plays. I have it tuned to a high frequency, so when I listen back, I can make sure I'm hitting the right tones, so it should work perfectly for this."

"You're amazing. Thank you," Silvia said.

"Yes, thank you," I chimed in, staring in wonder at how fast Silvia took action and put everything together while I moped.

"Okay, guys, it's showtime," Jen said with a dazzling smile before she sashayed over to the corner table.

Silvia gathered up her purse and slipped from her stool.

"Where are you going?" I asked, not ready to lose her emotional support.

"I'm going to see if I can sit closer and covertly record a video for backup. Besides, I love watching my woman work. It turns me on," she admitted.

I grimaced. "I'll pretend I didn't hear that."

She snickered, "Just like I'll try to pretend you're not salivating over Emma the next time she's sitting at our family table."

It was agony not going over to spy on Mr. Carter and Andrew, but something told me I needed to trust my sister and Jen. I also needed to warn Emma about her father's presence.

Before I could talk myself out of it, I fired off a quick text.

Jaime: I thought you'd like to know your dad is in The Lounge.

My phone buzzed in my pocket a couple of minutes later. A trill of anticipation ran through me, but her response merely said, "Thank you."

I wouldn't let myself read into the curt response. I'd given her a heads up, but now I needed to complete the mission and get proof of her father's deceitful acts.

Emma

♥

"Not to sound like a snob, but is this really the fanciest restaurant in Silverpine?" Caroline asked, looking around dubiously at all the wood-paneled walls.

I shrugged. "Well, yeah, outside the resort. Why? What's wrong with it?"

"Nothing," she said quickly, still looking around. "I've just never been in a fine dining establishment that had so many … antlers."

I rolled my eyes. "I'm sorry it doesn't live up to your fancy LA standards."

Caroline laughed. "Please, it's not like I've been able to enjoy anything LA has to offer lately. Most of my meals are enjoyed from the comfort of my office chair."

I was grateful for the opportunity to change the subject. The last few days, my mind had been consumed with how I would approach my father. I hoped by the end of dinner I would have a concrete plan.

"I'm sorry they've been running you ragged, Caroline. Have you decided what you're going to do about the job?" I asked.

Her painted lips twisted into a smile. "To be perfectly honest, the decision might be out of my hands. It's very possible they're drawing up my exit paperwork as we speak."

I looked at her, confused. "Why would they do that?"

She sighed, then let out a small laugh. "The other day, after our powwow with Sophie and you and I killed that bottle of wine, I got a text. I guess my boss didn't notice my name was still on the text chain, so he asked if anyone had heard from me and wanted to know, and I quote, *'How Caroline's mental breakdown was progressing?'* It was followed by a bunch of laughing/crying emoji."

I gasped on my friend's behalf. "That's so unprofessional."

"Tell me about it. Normally, I would've just taken a screenshot and sent it to HR, but I had a little too much alcohol in me, so I responded to the text … "

"Oh, no, do I even want to know?"

She rolled her eyes. "Probably not. If I was going to get fired, I wished it would've been a snappier comeback, but instead I told him my mental breakdown was progressing nicely, and I was doing better than his hairline."

My hand flew to my mouth, covering the laugh before it escaped.

She shook her head at me, smiling wryly. "I know. It was stupid. But part of me hopes they're working on that paperwork. Then I wouldn't have to make this decision."

"You know you could start your own firm, Caroline. You're the best financial planner I know, and I'm sure we can get you the backing. If things weren't so weird with my father, I'd just give you a job at the resort."

She waved a hand at me. "Don't worry about it right now, Emma. I'm not. Being away from LA and, more specifically, away from my desk, is reminding me I have a lot of life to live, and I've been doing a shitty job of it lately. I've really enjoyed slowing down and hanging out with you. It's making me seriously question what I'm even going back to."

I sighed. "I know what you mean. It's been nice being here."

I felt my phone buzz. "It's Jaime," I told Caroline. "He's warning me Dad is in The Lounge."

Caroline shook her head. "I wish I could say I'm surprised Daddy Moneybags showed up. But hopefully, it makes you feel less guilty about taking this meeting."

"I don't feel guilty. It just sucks it had to get to this point. I mean, he's the only family I have."

Caroline reached her hand across the table and grasped mine. "He may be blood, but you still have a family who loves you," she reminded me, squeezing my hand.

"Why such long faces on two beautiful ladies," a voice said, and we looked up to see a smartly dressed man wearing browline glasses.

"Emma Carter, I presume?" the man said, holding out his hand. I stood, shaking his hand, feeling relief course through me.

"Yes. You must be Mr. McCoy?"

He smiled at me widely. "At your service. And please, call me Connor. I apologize for being tardy. Traffic getting out of DIA was a bear and so was the driver if you know what I mean. I should've gotten his number now that I think of it," he said, looking thoughtful for a moment before shaking his head. "Now," he said, taking his seat and putting his briefcase aside. "I don't want to waste any of your time because I charge by the hour, so let's get down to business," he said, folding his hands in front of him and glancing at Caroline and me intently.

I cleared my throat, looking over at Caroline, and she nodded, urging me to go ahead. Connor was the bulldog Sophie had sent me. She'd assured me he was the best mergers and acquisitions attorney money could buy, and he was the guy we wanted in our corner. He was younger than I'd expected, but very attentive as I laid out the situation with my father.

When I finished, Connor didn't say anything for a long moment, drumming his fingers on the table as he looked thoughtful before he finally spoke. "If I understand correctly, you are a majority shareholder in the company?"

I nodded.

"Then he would definitely have a fight on his hands if you decide to go against him. If he's smart, and I have to believe he hasn't gotten this far in business relying purely on his good looks, then his legal team would take a meeting with me. From there, I should be able to shake him down to get off your back. But, Miss Carter, I have to warn you, I've been doing this a long time, and people can get nasty when they're desperate. And from what you've shared with me today, your father sounds pretty desperate. I want you to be prepared for the worst," he cautioned.

"Like what?" Caroline asked, never one to stray away from the dirty details.

"That he may launch a smear campaign, and you need to be prepared to do the same. I hope it doesn't go that far, but we need to be prepared. However, if that's how this goes, I don't see there being any issues on your end, Miss Carter," he said, looking at me earnestly. "You're a grieving daughter trying to honor her mother's wishes. You want to preserve the land and a town's way of life. You're the hero here, so in the court of public opinion, you win by landslide. These days, that's all that matters. Public opinion can put enough pressure on your father to make him back off. But in the meantime, I would suggest hiring security to run interference on your land, sending a clear message that trespassing of any kind will be met with consequences."

I sucked in a breath. "That I can do."

"I'm sorry, but that's it?" Caroline asked. "There aren't any injunctions or restraining orders we can file?"

Connor smiled at her. "You've been watching *Law and Order*, haven't you? At this time, no. Mr. Carter has been acting aggressively enough on his own, and it's my job to give him enough rope to metaphorically hang himself. If we return his aggression, it could backfire on us. Having a little patience is the best play here," he explained, and with that sentiment, I knew I liked Connor. My mother would've liked him, too.

"My job," Connor continued, "is to observe and un-cover their weak spots, so we can shut this down swiftly. I can assure you, I'm very good at observing details others don't see."

Caroline raised a curious eyebrow. "Oh, yeah? You'll have to forgive my cynicism, Mr. McCoy, but my friend here has been through a lot. It's going to take more than just your word that you're good at what you do."

Connor eyed her carefully, a smile playing at the corner of his lips. "Fair enough. Would it surprise you to know I noticed how you two were comforting each other when I walked in here? Or how the lumberjack at the bar has been undressing you with his eyes all night?"

Caroline's eyes widened. "I'm sorry, what?"

Connor kept his eyes on us and continued with an amused smile. "Eleven o'clock, tall, dark, and handsome with a beard. He's not been able to take his eyes off you, and from what I can see, he's more than just undressing you with his eyes. If I had to venture a guess, he's performing disgustingly heterosexual acts with you in his head."

I peered over Caroline's shoulder and breathed out, "Whoa, Caroline. He's right."

Caroline froze in her seat. "Well, now I've got to see him, but I can't turn around," she complained.

"Drop your napkin," Connor said helpfully, and Caroline followed his suggestion, bending down and glancing over her shoulder before righting herself. She looked back at us with flushed cheeks.

"You're good," she said to Connor.

"The power of observation, ladies. Everybody thinks they're good at it, but they'd be wrong. I'm the best. Now I could provide you with all the details I gathered about the other guests I observed as I walked in here, but I don't want to bore you with that. I would enjoy a drink though, and seeing as I'm an ethical attorney, I'll officially stop the clock on our business meeting. Now, does a place with this much wood and flannel have a bottle of Chardonnay, or am I going to need to slum it?"

I looked at Caroline. Mr. McCoy definitely delivered.

I tried to relax and enjoy the rest of the evening, drinking with Caroline and my new friend and lawyer, Connor, but I was not looking forward to going back to the resort, especially knowing my father was there. But our guest was tired, so we called it a night. Mr. McCoy would stay in a comped room at the resort, but he advised us to take separate cars. He didn't think it was a good idea for anybody to know he was representing me just yet.

Caroline and I left the restaurant shortly after she put a crick in her neck, looking over her shoulder to check out the lumberjack who'd been eyeing her all night.

"I mean, he's not really my type. But it's nice to be looked at like that, you know what I mean?" she said as we walked back into the resort.

This time, I couldn't help myself. My eyes went toward the bar, and I saw Jaime standing there, his eyes glued to me. Part of me wanted to talk to him, but I felt like I needed to get a better handle on the situation before we talked it out. I needed him to understand I could take care of things—that I didn't want to be his damsel in distress.

I looked away when I heard my father's familiar voice from the elevators. "And she returns," he said jovially enough, but I could hear the undercurrent of anger and irritation in his voice. He didn't like it when I challenged him.

"Father," I said, smiling tightly, "I'm surprised to see you here."

"Are you?" he asked as we approached, and he nodded in acknowledgment of Caroline. "Nice to see you again, Miss Sullivan. At the risk of sounding rude, may I have a private moment with my daughter?"

Caroline looked at me, asking with her eyes if I would be okay, and I nodded. "I'll be in the bar," she said, backing away.

Once she was out of sight, I faced my father. "You didn't have to come all the way out here, Dad," I maintained.

He scoffed. "Please, once I got wind of your behavior, I knew I'd have to make a trip here eventually, and then after our little conversation last night, I decided it couldn't wait."

I couldn't hold back the laugh. "My behavior?"

He shook his head sadly. "I don't know what's gotten into you, Emma. Your mother and I didn't raise you to behave this way—carrying on when you should be working—with someone way below your station, no less."

I rolled my eyes. "Father, please, who I choose to spend my free time with has no bearing on my position in the company."

"It sure as hell does when it's the difference between this company flourishing or failing."

I looked at him, confused. "Why would it make a difference? What are you not telling me?"

"Nothing you need to know. Besides, it will be none of your concern soon enough."

"What? Are you going to push me out? Have you forgotten I'm a majority shareholder?"

He shrugged his shoulders. "I have a feeling once the board hears about your philandering, they'll have no problem voting you out."

I glared at him.

"Don't give me that look, Emma. I have tried with you, I really have, but I'm down to my wit's end, and I will not have you tarnishing this company or your mother's name."

"Don't gaslight me," I hissed out. "We both know expanding onto that land is not what she would've wanted—and I will not allow it to happen."

"We'll just see about that young lady. I warned you before you're playing with the big boys now, so I hope you're prepared for what's ahead. I really don't want to use these tactics against my own daughter, but I am prepared to take what's rightfully mine."

"Go ahead and try, old man. Mom left that land to me, and I'm going to protect what's mine, including her legacy. That also includes the bartender you keep threatening. You seem to forget I'm not just Lydia Carter's daughter—I have just enough of your nastiness running through my veins to bite back, so maybe you should worry about fighting with the big girls."

With that, I turned on my heel and marched toward the bar. I couldn't walk in there, not when I was this upset. I didn't think Jaime would be so callous as to say I told you so, but I couldn't handle the pity in his eyes either.

I kept my gaze focused on Caroline, and she made a hasty exit. We rushed to the elevator and went to her room instead of mine. I rang my newly appointed lawyer and told him about the incident, and he cackled with glee. "Oh, I'm sorry, Emma. I'm not laughing at your expense. That is horrible. What a God-awful man. But I can tell you right now from a lawyer's perspective, he's going to be easy to squash, and I'm going to thoroughly enjoy it."

I wish I could say that made me feel better, but seeing the venom in my father's eyes shook me to the core.

I wasn't sure if I wanted to scream or cry, but we were interrupted by an incoming FaceTime call. It was Sophie, wanting to know how the meeting with the lawyer went. I was thankful for the distraction and happy when we got sidetracked talking about the amorous lumberjack at the restaurant bar. And yet as we laughed about Caroline's being ogled so thoroughly, my mind kept going back to Jaime. This situation was getting out of hand, and all I wanted to do was talk to him.

The voices were warring in my head. So what if I didn't have everything sorted? Of all people, he would understand, and he wouldn't judge me. Still, I couldn't help but want to go to him victoriously and let him know

I had fixed it. But perhaps more than anything, I just wanted him to hold me.

Jaime

♥

The last person I expected to see was Caroline, but when I saw her at the bar after walking in with Emma, I immediately felt comforted. She gave me a sympathetic smile. "Hey there."

Before she could get another word out, I asked, "Is she okay? Her father's here. She knows that, right?"

She nodded. "Yeah, thanks for the heads up. I think she suspected he was on his way, but still nice to know."

"She's out there alone with him?" I inquired.

Caroline smiled. "She is, but our girl's got this. I told her I was here to help, not that she needs either of us to rescue her."

I sucked in a breath. "I know I just …"

"You're a fixer, I get that."

I nodded. "That, and … we've been through this before," I confessed.

She nodded. "I get that, too, but she's not a kid any-more, and neither are you. You're both equipped to do it better this time. You're going to have to trust her."

Her words hit hard, but they weren't untrue. That was when Emma appeared in the bar's entryway looking for Caroline, presumably because she was avoiding looking at me.

Caroline glanced back at me. "I've got this. Have faith in our girl," she said, and I nodded, everything in me wanting to go after her to make sure she was okay. But Caroline was right. I needed to trust she could handle this on her own. It wasn't that I didn't think she was smart or tough enough to handle the situation. I just didn't want her to have to do it by herself. But family matters were complex, and the showdown between her and her father was a long time coming.

I understood why she had to do this on her own, but I was still going to help in any way I could. Which was why Silvia and Jen hid away in my office, going over the audio Jen recorded while sitting at the table with Emma's father and Andrew Travers Jr.

Charlie popped out from the back. "Hey, Jaime, you're needed in your office," he said as he took my place behind the bar.

This was it. Silvia and Jen could have in their possession the undeniable proof. When I walked into the small office, my sister's expression was strained, and Jen looked at me sympathetically.

"Well?"

"Oh, they sang like canaries," Jen said. "I wasn't expecting them to be quite so … forthcoming."

The knot of dread was back in my belly. "What do you mean?"

"I—um, well, he talked about his plans to expand on the land, bragged about it actually," Silvia said. "But I'll say Ashley was right. That man is a pig. Just listen for yourself," she said as Jen played the recording through the desktop's speakers.

"Now, tell me something. What was your name again? Uh, Jen?" John Carter's voice came through the speakers.

"I don't think I'm being unreasonable. I'm just being an effective businessman. This newer generation, present company excluded, of course, this new generation is so involved in feelings and creating lasting connections, and it gets in the way. You know, back in my day, it was about surviving and meeting needs. Now, my wife, she was a good woman, but I don't think she was impractical enough to think I wasn't out there getting my needs met."

Her nervous laughter wove through the speakers, and then Jen asked, "You described your wife as this beautiful and accomplished woman. Are you trying to tell me weren't getting your needs met at home?"

Mr. Carter laughed. "Of course, I was, but I was on the road a lot, and I'm sure you can understand sometimes the art of the deal isn't as simple as mouths talking. Sometimes, other parts have to talk if you know what I mean," he stated suggestively.

My stomach turned as I plopped down in one of the office chairs, and Jen and Silvia eyed me warily.

"So, you would fool around?" Jen asked.

"Oh, I wouldn't call it that so much as taking care of business. Now that's where you'll need to tread lightly," he said, presumably addressing Andrew. Mr. Carter continued, "My daughter is a smart woman, but she's like any other woman. No offense, of course, Jen. They get swept up by their emotions, so she may not be as understanding about what you'll be required to do to close deals. They don't understand there's nothing personal about it. It's just physical. A man needs to do what a man needs to do. That's why it's best to just keep that under your hat. I know everyone encourages couples to be open, but I never found it to be a good idea." Then there was mixed laughter.

I can only imagine my expression because Jen stopped the recording, and Silvia rushed to say, "I'm sorry. I know you were looking for a damming confession, and this sure as hell is one, but you're getting a little more than you bargained for."

"Yeah, your sister and I have been trying to figure out a way to splice this, so it only talks about the land deal, but he spent so much time bragging about his exploits it's impossible to separate it."

Silvia looked at me, concerned. "Do you think Emma has any idea? I mean, I know she's figured out he's a jackass, but the cheating is something else entirely."

I shook my head. "No, I'm pretty sure she has no idea. I don't think she would've been able to defend him as long as she has if she knew he was out there doing this to her mother. For all of his faults, she always insisted he was deeply in love with Mrs. Carter."

"He has a funny way of showing it," Jen muttered.

"What are you going to do?" Silvia asked.

I shook my head. "I don't know. I wanted proof—and I got it—but I can't imagine breaking her heart like this."

Silvia sighed. "I don't envy you, Jaime. I really don't. I have a feeling Emma will figure this all out anyway. Secrets have a way of coming out, but maybe she'll find out without having to hear about her father's infidelity."

I nodded. "Yeah, I hope that's the case," I said before rising from my chair. I smiled at Jen and my sister. "I can't thank you enough for helping me today. I don't know how I'll ever repay you."

"Please, getting to take down a dickhead is always a joy," Jen said with a wide smile. "Plus, your sister got to watch me work, so that was an added benefit."

"You were marvelous, my dear," Silvia said, smiling at her girlfriend.

"Let me take you out for dinner to repay you. Silvia, I'll call you later to set it up. But right now, I need to get back to work."

Both women nodded at me, understanding. They knew I wasn't just escaping—I had a decision to wrestle with.

When I returned to the bar, Mr. Carter was alone at the corner table, and I knew there was no holding back my disdain now.

He lingered for a while before wandering up to the bar, giving me an oily smile. "Bartender, I have to compliment your cocktails."

I nodded, "Thank you."

"But as good as you are at making a drink, I can see you still haven't learned your lesson. Hanging around my little girl as if you actually have a chance. I would think someone who valued their job would know well enough to stay away from the boss's daughter."

I bit back the retort on my tongue, wanting to oust him about the intel we'd just gathered, but it wasn't the time or the place, and I knew that.

So I gave him a tight smile. "I would think you'd appreciate that I value your daughter's safety and happiness above all else … sir," I bit off the last word. "Because she's worth it. I'm a faithful man, and I have faith Emma will see what kind of man you really are."

John Carter laughed, and it sent chills down my spine. "You know I can't fire you on the spot because it would be an HR nightmare, but you can bet your ass I'm working on it. One toe out of line, and you'll be out of here so fast your head will spin."

I smiled genuinely, and it seemed to unnerve him. "But I'll still have Emma."

His expression soured, and he banged a fist on the bar. "We'll see about that," he warned before storming out.

I knew I shouldn't have said that. I was definitely putting the cart before the horse, but I couldn't help but enjoy getting under his skin.

Now I just had to make sure my words wouldn't come back to bite me in the ass and that I would keep Emma by my side no matter how this went down.

Emma

I must've looked pensive after our call with Sophie, because Caroline huffed an exaggerated sigh. "If you're waiting for the perfect moment, Emma, I can assure you it doesn't exist—just go."

I didn't need her to clarify. I knew exactly what she was telling me to do. Truthfully, I needed very little encouragement. I missed him so much. Even though I was still in the thick of it with my father, I needed his support. I wanted him by my side.

I gave Caroline a quick hug and rushed out the door, hoping I wouldn't run into my father in the halls of the hotel.

Thankfully, it was late enough I saw very few people on my way to the bar. When I poked my head in the entryway, I could see it was mostly empty. They would call "last call" soon, and guests were already settling their tabs for the evening.

Jaime was hunched over the bar, focusing on the ledger in front of him, so he didn't notice me right away.

He looked tired, with dark smudges beneath his eyes, and I hated I'd caused that. But I wanted to make things right, so I squared my shoulders and marched over to him. When he looked up and saw me, a smile tugged at his lips.

"Emma, I'm so glad to see you. Listen, I'm sorry that—"

I held up a hand to stop him.

"Jaime, please. I'm the one who needs to apologize. Being back in Silverpine has been so painful … and surprisingly beautiful because of you. I shouldn't have pushed you away. It's been really hard for me to accept my father isn't who I wanted him to be—or needed him to be. I feel so ashamed."

"You have nothing to be ashamed of. You're not him, and you aren't responsible for his actions."

"Maybe not, but I feel responsible for letting him bully me into leaving you years ago. It hurt like hell, and I've missed you so much, but what hurts more is the idea that I caused you pain. I could justify my sacrificing to make my parents happy, but I can't justify you having to pay for it, too."

I reached across the bar and grabbed his hand. "I don't know if I'll ever forgive myself, Jaime, and I feel like I was falling into it all over again. There have been so many times I've wanted to tell my father to stick it where the sun don't shine, but he always played the mother card. When she first got sick, he told me if I continued seeing you, he would make sure I never saw my mom again. That he'd send her for treatment far away, and I believed him."

Jaime let out a low curse. "That son of a bitch."

"I know everybody thinks I've taken this too far and stayed loyal to him for too long, but I had to protect what was my mother's. I was all she had, and with my dad running around, screwing every woman in town, I felt like I needed to make it up to her somehow. I had to make sure her sacrifices to keep our family together weren't in vain. But I've realized she wouldn't want this life for me.

"She only ever wanted me to be happy, and I don't think she'd want me to sell my soul just to protect her family's land. I'm tired of being a pawn in my father's silly game. It's left me lonely and miserable, and I want my life back. A life with you if you can ever forgive me."

Jaime rushed around from behind the bar and swept me into his arms. I let out a cry of relief as he held me tightly. I didn't even feel the tears streaming down my cheeks, but when I leaned back, he swiped them away with his thumbs. "Bella, don't cry. I want to build a life with you, too. And I don't blame you for any of it. Your father took advantage of your warm, generous heart, and he'll pay for what he's done."

I gave him a watery smile, looking up into those chocolate brown eyes that were my home. "My only regret is I wanted to come here to tell you I had a plan, that it was all settled, and he'd no longer bother us. But I'm still figuring it out. I hired an attorney to help me fight fire with fire, but I need more proof he's going against my mother's wishes."

Jaime's brow raised. "Emma," he started. "You said you knew about him cheating on your mom, right?"

I nodded. "Unfortunately, everybody knew. It was embarrassing."

"That makes what I have a little easier to hand over. I wasn't trying to meddle, I swear. I just wanted the fucker to suffer after everything he put you through. Silvia and I hatched a scheme, and her girlfriend Jen stepped up to help us."

My eyebrows raised. "A scheme?"

"What would you say if I told you I caught your dad red-handed on tape bragging about expanding the resort on to *your* land?"

I looked at him in surprise. "I would say my lawyer would have a field day, and it would make things a lot easier."

"Then my job here is done," he said with a wink.

I yanked Jaime's mouth down to mine, needing to taste him again and not caring if his staff could see us. He leaned into it, holding me to him as if he'd never let me go, and that was a feeling I wouldn't take for granted ever again.

When we finally broke apart, gasping for air, he was smiling at me, and I could feel the grin overtaking my lips.

"Bella," he said in a ragged voice. "I'll be shutting down in a few minutes. What do you say I bring up a bottle of our best, and we celebrate?"

I couldn't help but tease, "What exactly are we celebrating, Jaime?"

He growled. "That we love each other, and I'm never letting you go ever again. That no one can come between us. It's you and me against the world."

I reached up and kissed him thoroughly once again before breathing against his mouth. "That sounds perfect. It'll give me just enough time to slip into something a little more comfortable," I said seductively, thinking of the slinky negligee I'd impulsively picked up a couple of days ago when Caroline and I had been out shopping.

Despite not knowing how it would all turn out, when I saw it on the mannequin it screamed, "Jaime would rip me off," and I had to scoop it up just in case. Now was the perfect time to wear it.

His smile widened, and heat overtook his eyes. "I'll take you any way I can get you. You look great no matter what you wear."

I laughed. "Yeah, I think you'll enjoy what I have in mind much better," I said, kissing him again. "See you in a few minutes?"

He kissed me hungrily before saying, "I can't shut this place down fast enough."

Reluctantly, we let each other go, and I floated back to the elevator and up to my room.

I couldn't believe I'd wasted so much time. After all these years of thinking we could never be and that I had to sacrifice all in the name of family. Never again. Jaime was my family and I no longer felt like I was missing a piece of myself. I felt empowered and loved.

Tonight, we would continue getting to know each other, knowing the future was bright—no boogie man waiting for us on the other side. It was the beginning of our new life together.

Tomorrow, I would contact Connor and hand over the recording.

Once in my room, I made a beeline for the small gift bag that held my impulse purchase. I slipped on the slinky fabric and freshened myself up. Soon I'd answer the door for the love of my life, feeling sexy and desirable.

The material was a deep emerald silk with the cups in black lace. It hugged me in all the right places and had little straps that would be so easy for Jaime to rip off. The thought sent wet heat spiraling through my core.

I'd just finished tucking a stray strand of hair back in place when I heard a knock at the door. My pounding heart went into overdrive. It was silly. It wasn't like it was our first time, but it felt different.

I raced to the door, not even bothering to look through the peephole. I couldn't wait to launch myself into Jaime's arms. But when I yanked open the door, my excitement came skittering to a stop because it wasn't Jaime standing there. It was Andrew, looking determined and belligerent.

I tucked myself behind the door trying to conceal myself as I asked him, "Andrew? What are you doing here? It's late."

His words slurred as he began his rant. "I came here to collect what's owed to me."

Everything inside of me panicked, and I cursed myself. I didn't have my phone nearby, so I couldn't call for help. It was after midnight, so if I had to scream, I would wake up the entire floor. Maybe I could shove him out before it came to that.

"Promises were made, Emma. You understand that, don't you? And I don't like being lied to. Now your father owes me, and he can't seem to keep you in line. So I'm going to follow his advice—take charge and do it myself."

I swallowed hard. "Andrew," I said as calmly as I could, "I can see you're upset, and I understand, but perhaps this is a conversation we should have in The Lounge. We can discuss these promises my father made, and what we might do about them."

He shook his head. "Oh, no, no, no, I'm done talking. I'm done waiting around and being made a fool of."

Before I could respond, his hand flew toward my face and covered my mouth and nose. I stumbled backward and opened my mouth to scream, but before the sound could escape, darkness descended over me.

Jaime

As I was shutting down the bar, I phoned Maria to make sure everything was okay at home and to let her know I wouldn't be there tonight. I wanted to make sure I wasn't leaving her in a tough spot, but she quickly connected to the dots and squealed in delight. "I'm so, so happy for you, Jaime. We've got it covered here. Take your time."

I was done in record time and flew to Emma's floor with wings on my feet. My Bella. She was finally mine, really mine. And it wasn't just that she'd told me she loved me and wanted a life with me that made my heart soar. It was that we'd run into some challenges over the last few days, but we were able to overcome them. They hadn't destroyed us as they had before. It was a relief to know she and I could weather the storms.

But my euphoria came crashing down when I approached Emma's hotel room, and the door was standing open.

I stepped inside, calling out Emma's name, but she wasn't there. Her purse was still there. Her phone was lying on the coffee table. "Shit," I cursed, racing out of her room and back toward the elevator as I pulled out my phone and dialed the head of security.

When he answered, I barked into the phone, "Hey, Phil, we have a problem. It's Emma Carter. It looks like someone's broken into her room, and she's been taken. All her stuff is here, but the door is standing wide open."

Phil was doubtful. "Does it look like there was a struggle?" he asked as I punched the "L" on the elevator to get back to the lobby.

"No, but her purse is laying out in the open along with her phone. That's not like her. Something's wrong."

"Okay, calm down, Jaime. Maybe she just forgot to close the door."

The elevator door slid open, and I rushed down the hallway toward the back of the building where the security office was located—where our head of security would be sitting taking this call.

"No, Phil. I'm telling you something is fucking wrong. Pull up the footage," I insisted.

"Come on, Jaime. You know I can't pull up camera footage for every little worry. There has to be a good reason. Oh, wait a minute, can you hold on? Somebody else is here."

Steps away from his office, I screamed into the phone, "No, this cannot wait! This is an emergency!"

I hung up and started to dial 911 when I saw who was approaching Phil's office.

"Caroline?"

She rushed over to me. "Please tell me you've seen Emma. I went to check on her in her room, and the door was standing open, but all her stuff was there."

"I know. That's why I'm here. I'm trying to get this jackass to pull up the security footage."

"What in the actual fuck?" Caroline asked. "I'm calling 911," she said, yanking her phone out of her back pocket.

"Good idea. Let me deal with this dumbass," I said, storming into Phil's office. "We need to pull up that footage now!"

At the sight of two frantic people, Jay stopped arguing and tapped on his keyboard to pull up the footage of the top floor.

"It couldn't have been that long. I just saw her a few minutes ago," I said, helping him narrow down the time window.

"Okay, let me see," he said before his eyes widened. "Oh, shit." He looked up at Caroline. "You said you called 911, right?"

At his question, I rush behind the desk to look at the footage myself. There it was, plain as day—that fucker Andrew was dragging her lifeless form out of the room and then threw her over his shoulder like she was nothing more than a sack of potatoes.

I watched in horror, barely registering Phil barking orders into his walkie-talkie, dispatching all security guards to be on the lookout for Emma and the kidnapper, Andrew Travers Jr.

"You know him?" Caroline asked Phil.

"Yeah, Mr. Carter introduced me to him earlier when they were having a meeting and I passed by. Lucky I know his name."

"Yeah, lucky," she muttered.

"Listen, Jaime, that was only a few minutes ago. They couldn't have gotten far," Phil said.

My mind ran through the grounds of the resort that had been tattooed on my memory for twelve years. My father and I were part of building the place, and I knew every cranny. "There are plenty of places to hide in the hotel. But you'd buy yourself more time by taking her out of the hotel. Phil, is there any footage of him getting into a car?"

Jay's eyes returned to the computer. "That's what I'm looking for. I'm not seeing anything, but oh, wait, here we go. There's no footage because the cameras are blacked out, but one of the emergency exits on the east side has been triggered."

"East side? Heading toward …" I stopped. "The maintenance shed," I fumed. I looked over at Caroline. "You good here?"

"Yeah, I'll wait for the cops. Go find our girl," she said. I turned to go, and she called after me. "And Jaime, please be careful. She'll kill me if anything happens to you."

I gave her a nod and ran toward the maintenance shed, my heart pounding in my ears.

There was no way I would let that motherfucker get away with whatever he had planned for Emma. I wouldn't let him take her away from me or end things for us before they even began.

"I'm coming, Emma," I whispered as I ran out the back door of the resort.

Emma

My mouth felt like cotton, and everything was dark. There was a dull throbbing in my head, and even though my body felt like lead, I strained to hear and pick up the words floating over me.

The voice was frantic and hushed, and … were they crying?

Choked sounds came, and my ears tuned in to pick up snippets.

… "I'm sorry, Dad. I don't know how to fix this …"

… "I messed up bad. What do I do now?

… "I just wanted what was owed to me …"

Those last words flipped a switch inside me. Andrew.

That was right. He'd come to my room, rambling on about promises, then put that God-awful rag over my mouth, and it was lights out for me.

What was I thinking just opening the door like? It was all coming back to me, and I realized the horrible situation I was in.

I flexed my fingers. They felt stiff, and I realized my hands were tied together behind my back.

Fuck.

I was still only in the nightie and nothing else, laid out on something hard.

I could see bits of light coming through a window, but I couldn't see Andrew. I just felt him pacing at my feet as he muttered into a phone.

I shut my eyes again, trying to concentrate on what I could figure out with my other senses.

I smelled … what was that smell? Motor oil? And wood shavings and outside?

We were in a building, but it didn't feel like a finished room.

Okay, Emma. You're going to have to gather your courage and start asking questions.

But what the hell did I ask a lunatic?

"Andrew?" My voice came out rusty.

"Oh, shit. I gotta go," he said, and then he was addressing me. My eyes could barely make out his silhouette looming over me in the dark.

"Where are we?" I dared to ask.

"Don't you worry about that," he snapped, "Not until I figure out what our next move is." I could see his shadow running a worried hand through his hair as he continued to pace.

"You know, it was never supposed to go this far, Emma. If you would have just cooperated ..."

I was silent for a moment as my brain scrambled to think of the right words to say that wouldn't get me killed. "You know," I stuttered out, "It's not too late to make things right."

He snorted. "Yeah, and how do you propose to do that? I mean, I just drugged a woman and kidnapped her. Not really sure how to come back from that, but I have to figure out something—my old man has been no help. "

"That's something I'm familiar with," I'm muttered.

"I know, I mean, they make all these promises, and then they just do whatever the fuck they want. As if there are no repercussions."

I nodded, but stopped when the movement sent a sharp spike of pain through my head. "We have that in common," I said, trying to keep him talking, hoping to calm him down.

"I know. You see? We're better suited than you thought. But you didn't want to give me a chance because of that stupid bartender. I told my dad he would be a problem. Anyone with eyes could see that."

"Andrew," I said, bringing attention back to me and away from Jaime, "Let's forget about our fathers for a moment because obviously neither one of them is interested in helping us. You and I are two capable adults. There's no reason we shouldn't be able to figure out a path here."

"That may be true for you," he said. "But it's too late for me."

I had to keep him talking. "No, it's never too late. What exactly did my father promise you?"

Andrew launched into details of our proposed marriage and merging the family businesses. How the new company would build boutique businesses off the back of the resort, and we would "make millions."

When he mentioned we would be expected to produce multiple heirs to inherit the family fortune, I swallowed back the bile rising in my throat.

But he was talking, and as long as he continued, I could test the strength of my restraints. They didn't seem impossible to get out of. I tried to keep him talking as I carefully worked my wrists out of the restraints.

He was complaining about how his father had never seen him as anything other than incapable when he paused. "What do you think you're doing?" he asked tersely.

I sucked in a breath. "I'm having a conversation with you. We're sorting out this mess."

"No. No, you're just trying to play me like the rest of them so you can get out of here … And then what? Tell me, Emma, what happens when you leave here? Are you going to act like this didn't happen?"

I swallowed hard before I said, "I can keep a secret if you can."

He snorted. "Yeah, I don't believe you. Your father was right about one thing—women are conniving, and you have to watch them every step of the way. You're not going anywhere, Emma." As he closed the distance between us, there was a loud crash from the door being kicked down.

"Jaime!"

Jaime

I prayed to God my hunch was right.

When Phil said the emergency exit had been tripped, but the cameras were dark, I knew I was on the right track. The maintenance shed was tucked neatly away in the woods several hundred yards from the back of the resort. If he'd taken her around any other side of the building, the cameras would've picked it up.

My heart was pounding in my ears as I approached the dark shed. Emma must be terrified. As I grew closer, I slowed my steps, wanting to be as quiet as possible.

As I neared the shed, I could hear voices.

Jackpot.

I tried to listen to the conversation, but I couldn't pick up the words. Suddenly, I heard a male voice rise sharply, and I knew she must be in trouble.

I sucked in a breath and kicked in the door to reveal Andrew and Emma sitting in an awkward tangle on the floor, her hands tied behind her back.

She cried out my name when she saw me, but before I could get to her, Andrew launched himself at me. "You're not going to ruin this for me now," he spit out as I reached for him. I wrapped my hands around his throat as he tried to fight back.

He managed to pry one of my hands from his throat, but I just swung it back into his face, enjoying the sickening crack.

My hand would hurt like hell later, but I didn't care.

I had an advantage over Andrew because even though he was taller than me, I had rage on my side. I didn't even realize the litany of curses flying out of my mouth as I pummeled him.

Somehow in the tussle, Andrew got a hand to the back of my head and yanked on my hair, forcing one of my hands to release him. Then he had the advantage and knocked me to the ground. I heard Emma cry out, but I couldn't focus on that for too long because Andrew was towering over me.

Sprawled out on the ground, I reached out, feeling around for anything I could use as a weapon, and Andrew chuckled cruelly.

"Nice try, bartender," he said before leaning over me, his fist pulling back to punch me.

But before he could touch me, there was a sickening sound of metal against bone, and the son of a bitch collapsed on top of me.

I looked up to find Caroline with a shovel in her hands.

"Sorry for the awkward position here, folks," she said, noting how Andrew had fallen on top of me.

There was a myriad of shouts, then "Ma'am, let us through!"

Soon, police officers were removing a groaning Andrew from on top of me and putting handcuffs on him.

As soon as I was free of his weight, I scrambled to Emma, checking over her face and arms. "Bella, are you okay?"

Tears were streaming down her cheeks. "I'm okay. Just a nasty headache." She shifted toward me. "Would you mind getting my hands?"

As I reached behind her, a fresh wave of sickness rolled over me at the way she'd been bound, but I quickly undid her restraints. As soon as her hands were free, she threw them around my neck.

"Ma'am, I'm sorry to interrupt, but we need to ask you a few questions, and there's a paramedic on the way to check you out," a policewoman said.

Emma nodded in response as I held her to me, rocking her back-and-forth, not knowing what to say. Just feeling so grateful I found her.

"You scared the hell out of me, Bella," I said into her hair.

She hiccupped a laugh. "Don't worry, I scared the hell out of me, too."

There was a commotion on top of the other commotion outside as an officer read Andrew his rights. I heard a familiar but unwelcome voice, booming. "What the hell is going on here?" Mr. Carter's voice rang out, belittling Andrew. "What do you think you're doing, son?"

By now Andrew had come to, still groaning. He responded, "I only did what you suggested."

Emma and I looked at each other in horror, and I moved to the doorway of the shed to hear more clearly as Mr. Carter lowered his voice and hissed, "I suggested no such thing. I just told you to scare her a little. You took this way too far."

Rage rushed through me, and even though there was a voice in me that cautioned to behave around the officers, another voice urged me to get in Mr. Carter's face and tell him exactly how I felt about how he'd treated his only daughter.

But once again, someone else was quicker than I was. The next thing I knew, Caroline was charging at Mr. Carter, kneeing him squarely in the nuts.

He doubled over, groaning. "Sick fuck," she hissed. "How could you do this to your own daughter? What the fuck is wrong with you?"

An officer came to restrain Caroline, telling her to calm down and take a breath.

Mr. Carter looked up and snarled, "What are you doing? Arrest her. You just saw her assault me."

The officer he belittled looked at him lazily. "I'm sorry, sir. I have no idea what you're talking about."

Another officer emerged to lift Mr. Carter from the ground and put him in cuffs.

"Get these off me. Why are you cuffing me? I haven't done anything wrong."

"Sir, Mr. Travers says otherwise. He claims you're his accomplice, so we're going to take you both down for questioning and sort this all out."

Mr. Carter was seething, and I bit back a laugh before looking at Caroline and complimenting, "That was amazing."

She smiled. "It felt pretty amazing."

I turned back to Emma, who was crying, and my smile instantly fell. "He was in on it," she croaked.

"Oh," I sighed, rushing to her and gathering her in my arms. "Emma, I'm so sorry."

She cried into my shoulder. We stayed like that for a long moment until a paramedic announced, "We're going to need to check on everybody and make sure you're all okay."

We welcomed them in, and they helped Emma to a standing position and checked her out in the back of the ambulance.

She was okay, but they said someone would need to watch her sleep to make sure she didn't experience any side effects from the drug Andrew used to knock her out.

I volunteered, and they gave me a list of symptoms to watch out for, and then she was released to me.

Understandably, Emma didn't want to go back to the Carter family suite, so Caroline quickly produced the card to her room and said she would go to Emma's room and gather her things to bring to us.

"I don't know how I'll ever repay you, Caroline," I said.

She smiled. "Just take care of her," she said before she was interrupted by a police officer asking for a statement.

I didn't leave Emma's side as she gave her statement to the officers.

The police were appalled. Of course, it was a small town, and they knew John Carter and Emma even though she hadn't been around for a while.

As the policewoman finished up with our statements, she clucked her tongue and gave us a sympathetic smile. "I'm sorry you had to go through this, Miss Carter. I knew your mama. She was a good woman and kind to everyone she ever met. It's a real shame she was stuck with that snake."

"My sentiments exactly." I replied.

I took Emma back to Caroline's room to rest.

She assured me she was fine and didn't think she'd be able to sleep. She just wanted to stay up and lie in my arms. The statement warmed but also concerned me. I couldn't get her to stop shaking, no matter how tightly I held her. Despite her insisting she'd never be able to sleep, less than five minutes later, she was passed out.

I stayed awake, not wanting to miss a moment or anything that might indicate she was having an adverse reaction to the drugs.

That son of a bitch actually drugged her. It was so evil and unbelievable, and yet here we were.

Emma was still asleep in the early morning hours as the sunrise filtered through the drapes. By then, everyone in town had heard about the arrest of the larger-than-life John Carter.

I had to give the residents of Silverpine credit. From what I gathered from the posts on social media, they didn't hold back on the details or paint him out to be some sort of misunderstood figure.

Soon, my sisters called, as did Charlie. They were all worried about Emma and me.

I tried to stay quiet as I explained the situation to Silvia and Maria simultaneously. "We're fine. I'm keeping an eye on her … we're going to get through this."

"I'm just so glad you thought of that maintenance shed. If you'd waited for the police, it might have been too late."

"No kidding," Maria chimed in. "And you need to introduce me to Caroline. She sounds fabulous."

I laughed. "Yeah, it's a relief to know Emma has such good friends. I know she's more than capable of taking care of herself, but it's still comforting."

"Now she has even more family to watch over her whether she likes it or not, and I'm pretty sure all of Silverpine will be rooting for Emma, too. Listen, Jaime, I know you probably want some time for yourselves, but the next few weeks are going to be challenging, especially once charges are filed. People are going to be asking us how they can help, so think about what you and Emma might need to get through this, okay?" Silvia said, ever practical about the realities that would face us in the coming weeks.

My sister's concern wasn't surprising, but I still choked up.

"Jaime," Maria said softly, "it's okay to let it out. You've been through a lot. Just remember, you'll always have us, and we're going to help you and Emma through this as a family."

I choked out, "Thank you. That means the world to me. I'm not even sure why I'm crying—it's probably the adrenaline crashing," I said, hoping my sisters would understand it wasn't just the night before making me so emotional. But it was twelve years of feeling adrift without Emma. We had a hell of a time getting back to each other, but she was here now, and I felt like I could breathe again.

"Jaime?" Emma's scratchy voice drifted up from beside me.

"Hey, she's waking up. I gotta go," I told my sisters.

"Give her our love. We'll check in on you later. Love you," they said in near unison.

"I love you more," I said, before hanging up and turning to Emma.

"That was Maria and Silvia. They were checking up on you, and they promised to give us some space, but realistically, that means we only have a few hours before they show up with a casserole," I grinned.

Emma smiled sleepily at me. "How long have I been out?"

I looked at the clock. "Almost twelve hours."

"Did you get any sleep?"

"Who needs sleep when there's a goddess spread out next to me?"

She sighed. "You must be exhausted," she said as she tried to sit up. I leaned over to help her as she hissed and grabbed her head. "It's okay, I'm fine. I just … I can't believe that actually happened. I've been fighting my instincts about my father for so long, but I never thought he'd take it that far."

"I'm so sorry, Emma."

She wouldn't let me continue. "No, I'm the one who's sorry. I wasted so much time. We could've had all this time together."

I captured her face gently in my hands. "We can't think about it like that. We went out and lived our lives, made mistakes, and learned lessons so we could come back together and appreciate how special what we have is."

She leaned her face into my hand. "I hope you know I don't intend to let you go, not in this lifetime."

"Promise?" I said, feeling warmth flood through me.

"I promise," she said before leaning forward and kissing me.

The kiss was gentle, but it was just as fervent and meaningful because it was the kiss that would officially start our forever.

"I love you so much, Jaime."

"I love you more," I said, leaning down and kissing her.

I don't know how long we stayed like that, but we only broke apart when there was a knock at the door ... along with the sound of my sisters' voices and the telltale smell of an incoming casserole.

Epilogue

One year later …

"In the cases of Andrew Travers Jr. and Pine Crest Resort's John Carter, both defendants have filed appeals for new trials. Just a year ago, Silverpine was stunned by the horrifying news of the two men's crimes against one of the defendant's daughter, Emma Carter.

The community was outraged to learn John Carter helped plan the drugging and kidnapping of his daughter, intending to force her into marriage.

Carter and Travers are being held in the county jail until their transport to state prison next week …"

Sophie appeared before me, taking the TV remote from my hand and switching it off. "Okay, my friend, enough. Today is supposed to be a good day. We don't need Daddy Moneybags spoiling it."

I smiled at my friend, grateful she was here. Actually, both of my best friends were here for the ribbon-cutting of the new Lydia Carter Park, formally known as that big chunk of land that sat behind the resort.

After everything had gone down with my father and Andrew Jr., I'd decided it was time to do something with that land. My mother would have wanted people to have access to it, but not through strip malls and parking lots. She would want people to enjoy the beauty of it just like she did.

So, besides being appointed the new president and CEO of Pine Crest Resorts by the board of directors, Jaime and I had been busy working on the park, getting all the proper permits and installing walking trails, as well as hiring park rangers to patrol the land to make sure it stayed pristine.

Sophie and Caroline had arrived a couple of days before, and that day, we were having Sunday dinner with Jaime and his family. Well, my family, too.

It was the same house Jaime had grown up in, but now it belonged to Maria, her husband Carlos, and their baby girl, Esme.

Sadly, a few months after everything went down with my father, Jaime's mother passed away, but not before she got to hold of her first grandchild … named Esmeralda in her honor.

"I'm excited about tonight. I've been hearing about this Sunday dinner all year, and it's essentially the merging of two families," Sophie said.

I smiled at her fondly. "I'm excited about it, too. You and Caroline will hit it off with his sisters and," I drew out the word, "that means you would have even more friends if you were to, you know, move to Silverpine permanently."

Sophie rolled her eyes. "Not this again, Emma. Look, I know this is your home, and it's lovely to visit, but you're talking to a hard-core SoCal girl. Are you seriously trying to convince me snowy winters are a good thing? How am I supposed to acclimate to this?"

"Easy. One Christmas in the snowy mountains, and you'll be hooked, believe me. Call me selfish, but I want you here, and you both have been saying you need a fresh start. Plus, it'll give you some much needed space you've been saying you need from your mother."

Sophie growled. "Don't even get me started with her. She's hard to deal with on a good day, and now that it's election season, she's damn near unbearable. If you think she's going to let me go anywhere during an election year, you're out of your mind."

"Okay," I said, "I'll pester you again in six months."

She rolled her eyes. "Why don't you focus on Caroline? You have a better shot at getting her to move out here."

I wasn't sure about that. Caroline had gone back to her soul-sucking job in LA. She'd insisted she valued the security of being an employee over the uncertainty of starting her own firm.

But she'd been waffling since. She'd toyed with the idea of opening her own consulting firm, but something held her back. I felt like I was wearing her down to come work for Pine Crest Resorts, but I could tell part of her didn't like the appearance of nepotism even though she was the most qualified candidate I knew for the job.

Besides, the current CFO of Pine Crest was an old pal of my father's. He'd been grumbling about retirement, and I would be happy to get him out of here. It was time for a new guard in the C-suite, one that stood a more ethical ground.

"Where is Caroline anyway? She knows we have to leave soon," Sophie grumbled, checking her watch.

"She told me a couple of hours ago she was going for a walk."

Sophie stopped, looking at me with wide eyes. "A walk? Our Caroline?"

I laughed. "She said she wanted to check out the park after seeing all the improvements we made after the ribbon-cutting yesterday. Plus, I suggested it was a good way to clear her head."

Sophie nodded. "I wonder how many walks it's going to take for her to figure out she needs to quit that job."

"I don't know," I said, shaking my head. "But I hope she comes to that conclusion soon. I hate seeing her so unhappy."

"Seeing who unhappy?" Caroline said, breezing back through the hotel door.

She was slightly out of breath, and her hair was disheveled, and ... "Caroline? Are those twigs in your hair?"

She looked at me, startled. "Uh, maybe. Why?"

"Did you get into it with a bear out there or something?" Sophie teased.

A smile overtook Caroline's lips. "You could say that," she said, picking twigs out of her hair. "I apologize for being late. Let me go clean up, and then we can be on our way, ladies."

"Caroline? Why do you look like you just took a tumble in the hay?" I asked.

She shook her head, "I don't know what you're talking about ... now taking a tumble in the dirt ... maybe against a tree? That's a whole other matter."

"Wait. What? With whom?" Sophie gasped.

Caroline grinned at us. "That's the beauty of it. I have no clue. He was big, he was hot, and it was amazing."

Sophie and I had a plethora of questions, namely how Caroline went for a walk in the woods and ended up getting fucked against a tree.

"Look, before you guys start mothering me, I can assure you I was safe, and no plant life was harmed," she said, pointing to me. "We might've traumatized a few squirrels, but it's nature, so it's natural, right? "

Sophie and I looked at each other in shock. Caroline, our buttoned-up Caroline, was admitting to having sex in the woods.

We followed her into the bathroom as she fixed her hair.

"I have so many questions," Sophie said as we helped Caroline put herself back together to get ready for dinner.

On the ride to Maria's house, we got quite the story.

As soon as we arrived at Maria's house, Sophie and Caroline were instantly embraced, quite literally. Silvia and Maria hugged my best friends like they were long-lost sisters and were introduced to Esme as her new aunts.

Caroline looked at me, slightly alarmed, but I nodded to both of them. "Just go with it. This is good."

We took turns cuddling baby Esme. Jaime was convinced she would never learn how to crawl or walk because no one would set her down for more than two seconds.

But her chubby little cheeks and big brown eyes were hard to resist.

"I'm delighted you could come to Sunday dinner. We've been waiting a long time to meet you," Maria said as she set out dish after dish of steaming food.

"Same could be said for you two," Caroline said, smiling.

"Yeah, I think Mama would've loved this. New friends coming together as a family under her roof around her table."

"Yes, no doubt she's thrilled watching us right now because, more than having all of us here together, she wanted her children to be happy, and I think she got her wish," Silvia said, looking over to Jaime pointedly with a small smile playing her lips. "Well, almost, right, Jaime?"

I'd noticed when I walked in that Jaime was extra nervous, and I wondered why because he loved Caroline and Sophie, and Maria and Silvia were equally remarkable, so I didn't see why they wouldn't all get along famously.

But his sister's words were met with a nervous smile. "Right, that's my cue," he said, turning to me.

"Jaime? Is everything alright?" I asked, concerned.

"Not quite, but I think it will be," he said, a nervous smile still in place.

"It's been a big year with a lot going on, so it never seemed like the right time, but I don't want to wait any longer. Emma Carter, I don't want to spend another day not being your husband. You're the only woman I've ever loved and the only woman I will ever love. We were apart for so long, and I tried to move on, but I always knew deep down it was too late for me. My heart belonged to you, and I would remain yours, no matter what. And then fate brought us together again, and I won't be an idiot and throw this opportunity away. Spending the past year with you has been the best year of my life. The only thing that could make it better is if you would be my wife."

He got out of his chair and scooted it back, getting down on one knee and pulling a black velvet box out of his pocket. Snapping it open, I saw a beautiful princess cut solitaire set in white gold. Sharing this moment with our friends and family took my breath away.

"Jaime, of course, I'll be your wife! Now get up here and kiss me," I insisted, yanking at his shirt to get him off the floor.

Silvia urged him, "You heard the woman. Kiss her."

When our lips met, our family broke out into applause. I didn't even realize tears were streaming down my face until Jaime pulled away and wiped them away with his thumbs.

"You've made me the happiest man on the planet, Emma Carter," he whispered against my lips.

"You just wait, Jaime," I teased before kissing him again to whoops and hollers from our family.

"Get a room," Carlos goaded.

We stayed in our embrace for a long time. I wasn't about to let go of Jaime, never again.

Thank you for reading *Never Finished*.

If you liked this book, then you will love *Second Chance with My Ex's Brother*!

Why you'll love it...

* One night stand
* Age gap
* Off-limits
* Forced proximity
* Protective hero

Here's a sneak peek...

One night. No promises. No last names. Just raw passion.
The twist? He's my ex's brother.

I slipped away at dawn... never knowing who he was. Miles was my escape, a way to reclaim my fire and direction.

Our affair became a pivot point that altered my life's course forever.

Years later, I am the proud co-owner of a successful Sonoma winery...

And Miles is standing before me as a guest at the grand opening of my new resort—sexier than ever and still HOT for me.

His kiss still sears and I want to give in, but I will not be distracted. Everything I've worked for hangs in the balance.

When the rest of his family arrives, the puzzle pieces come together, and I question everything—including his love for me.

Can I forgive his omission, or will our past extinguish the hope of a second chance?

Scan to get *Second Chance with My Ex's Brother* now!

Sneak Peek Second Chance with My Ex's Brother

PAIGE

"Paige? Paige, what happened?" Mia asked, running after me as I stormed into our apartment, tears streaming down my cheeks.

I tried to speak, but it came out garbled, even to my own ears. Miraculously, Mia did not need a translation. We'd been best friends since we were eight and sometimes, I was sure we could read one another's minds.

"That lying son of a bitch! You were always too good for him," she hissed in response to my tear laden explanation of my boyfriend of a few months unceremoniously dumping me. The man who I was certain was "the one" had casually ended things. When I had the audacity to be upset, he turned nasty, telling me if I hadn't been such a "cold fish" then maybe he would have stayed interested.

Mia sat back. "Maybe Leo needs a reminder of what a cold fish really is. I say we start by shoving a bunch of supermarket fish in his tailpipe."

"Mia..." I drew out her name in warning.

"Oh! Oh, I know... stick a few beneath his mattress and turn up the heat," she suggested, her eyes lit up. "You still have his spare key, right?"

I bit back a laugh. Mia was stone cold serious—and that's why I loved her.

"I saw that laugh," she said in mock outrage. "Laugh all you want, but I'll be adding a few pounds of scrod to my online order tonight," she promised before slipping away to the kitchen.

I listened as she rummaged around in the kitchen. I found one shred of calmness that allowed me to dry my face with the sodden tissue I didn't even remember plucking out of the tissue box.

How had I not seen this coming? Leo had been growing distant, but I'd chalked it up to his intense studying for finals. I still had a couple of semesters left before I graduated from college, but this was Leo's last semester. He was about to take the LSATs, and it would determine what law school he would attend. He came from a long line of lawyers: his grandfather, father, and older brother were all practicing. There was an expectation that everyone in the Townsend family would practice law and Leo had been tearing his hair out for weeks preparing for the test.

I'd helped him with flashcards, timed practice tests, and scheduled study breaks with homemade meals to ensure his success. We'd even planned an end of the semester party together in anticipation of him passing. It was going to be a big blowout for him and all of his law school bound buddies at his parents' lake house. Actually, Leo had secured the lake house while I hustled to plan the entire party because he was busy studying. Mia had warned me I was doing too much. "You have your own finals to study for," she'd reminded me.

To which I replied, "I know, but this is an important night for us—one we will remember for the rest of our lives."

Soon after, when he'd met me after work to give me the good news that he'd passed the LSAT with flying colors, I launched myself at him with a congratulatory hug. I didn't understand the uneasy look in his eyes when he'd set me down away from him and told me we were over.

"I mean, really, fuck that guy. After everything you've helped him with. Not to mention you put all of your plans on hold for him. You even changed career paths because of him," Mia fumed from the kitchen as I stared at the wall. Sadly, she was right.

I wanted to get my degree in business. Running my own business sounded like fun. I hadn't been sure what kind of business that would be until shortly before Leo and I had gotten involved. I recently started working at a fancy restaurant on the opposite side of town. Not only were the tips great, but I no longer left work smelling like a greasy spoon like I had at my previous serving job. The restaurant, Bella Nova, took its menu seriously. So much so that the waitstaff was required to take a wine education course so we could recommend proper pairings with the dishes. I'd only just turned twenty-one when I took the job, so I knew nothing about wine. But in the last few months, I'd become intrigued and a little obsessed with the extensive process that went into creating an excellent wine.

When I mentioned my dream of opening a winery someday to Leo, he laughed. "You're telling me you're going to spend all your time learning about alcohol?"

"Well, yeah. It's a multi-million-dollar business if you can create a place for yourself. And I'm enjoying all the stuff I'm learning." I explained.

He smirked at me. I should've read that as a red flag and then he said, "sounds to me like you want to be a professional wino." I had taken it as a joke instead of the insult it was.

Leo was smart, and he held himself with such confidence that I never questioned him. Somewhere along the way, I'd lost myself and got swept up in the idea of being in a relationship and being loved.

I was so focused on being what I thought Leo wanted that I had let him talk me into changing my major. He convinced me I should work at his law firm with him—not as a lawyer, of course, because he wouldn't want to compete against his girlfriend. But he said they always needed mediators. I hadn't completely understood what the job entailed, but when he described to me, it sounded boring as hell. He sold it as something respectable and stable, so I had agreed. I had been fighting my way through the classes, trying not to fall asleep—all for nothing.

"This sucks," I said, from my place on the couch to Mia. "I mean, I met his whole family—well, most of his family. I never met his older half-brother. But I sent him a video message."

"You sent him a video message?" Mia asked, confused.

"Yeah, one time when I was at his parent's house, Leo's mom was worried because I guess his older brother had been having a hard time. So, she was going around recording everyone giving encouraging words to Wallace. But Leo couldn't be bothered, so she asked me to give him some encouraging words instead. I hadn't even met the guy, but she seemed happy with it."

"I bet his mom's going to be heartbroken over this one," Mia said.

"I know. I'm going to miss her. She was really nice. She made me feel like—like I was a part of the family."

Mia laughed. "I'm sure she wanted you to be part of the family… I don't know any mom her age, with a son, who doesn't look at you and think daughter-in-law material."

I swallowed around the fresh lump of emotion growing in my throat. Yet another thing that sucked about this whole situation. Even though Leo and I had only been together for a few months, things moved quickly. I had already gotten to know his parents, and I was supposed to meet his half-brother Wallace at graduation. That wouldn't be happening now. I'd spent the last few months thinking I was marching towards my happily ever after, and he snatched it away just like that.

Mia returned, this time with two steaming mugs of tea. I looked down at the murky liquid. "Don't worry, I put a little whiskey in there," she winked.

I smiled at her.

"It may not seem like it now, Paige, but you're better off without him. Somewhere out there is your knight in shining armor. I know it," she assured me.

"I wasn't looking for a knight in shining armor… I was hoping for a nice guy who would love me for me."

She nodded. "Well, Leo isn't that guy. But the right one is out there and we're young, so there's no rush."

I nodded in agreement. "You're right, as usual." I was feeling a little better after her pep talk when a text message alert on my phone chimed. I lunged for it, thinking it might be Leo and I was right. The words that met my eyes were not flowery words of regret and professed love. Instead, they read:

Hey, I know what went down between us is still a little raw, but would you mind getting a hold of the DJ for the party and asking him to be here an hour earlier?

I let out an angry sigh.

"Oh no, what does it say?"

I handed Mia the phone and watched her eyes nearly pop out of her head as she read the text. "The nerve of that asshole. I mean, he stomped on your heart and now he's worried about this stupid party."

"Yep. A party I drove myself to distraction over planning. Nit-picking every single detail instead of studying more for my finals," I fumed.

Mia looked at me for a moment, and then a wicked grin spread across her mouth. "The party you and I are going to crash," she said.

I sat up from the couch. "Oh, no, how humiliating would that be?"

"Not at all, and I'll tell you why. You're going to put on your sexiest dress and strut into that party like you own the place. He's going to realize how bad he fucked up, while you and I have a grand old-time dancing with cute guys."

I shook my head, recoiling at the thought of what she was suggesting.

"Come on, Paige," she pleaded. "I understand you're hurt, I do, but do you want to shrink away that easily? This guy needs to understand he can't behave that way. If he wanted to end the relationship, fine, but he could've had some compassion."

"You won't get any argument for me," I agreed.

"Think about it Paige, think about all the things you have changed and sacrificed for this guy. It's time to take it back."

As I plopped back down on the couch, a fresh wave of mortification rolling over me when I thought about all the changes I made to be a "better fit" for him. I had changed my major, my career path, and a hundred other little things to make him happy. Somewhere in all of that, I lost myself. I never used to twist myself into a pretzel to make somebody happy, but in my quest for love and companionship, I had turned into a complete doormat.

I'd watched my mother cater to my father's every whim. It was in those rare moments when we were alone that I experienced how vivacious and fiery she was. I remember being flabbergasted she wasn't naturally this mousy, subservient woman. But after so many years with my father, she had folded herself into what she thought was a much more palatable version of herself, at least for him.

It made me resent him and his bullishness, and I had wondered why she had stayed with him. By the time I left for college, I had accepted that people stayed in relationships for their own reasons and it was between the two of them. She was an adult, and as much as it broke my heart to watch her hide her sassy side, I knew I had to continue to be the force of nature she raised me to be. For both of us. Then I met Leo…

It's not like he asked me to change everything about myself. I just followed the example I was shown my whole life.

"Wait a minute, what's going on here?" Mia said, waving her hand in front of my face. I pulled myself out of my contemplation and looked at her with determined eyes.

"I had a major epiphany," I said, feeling the strongest I had in a long time.

"Oh? Tell me," Mia said with raised eyebrows.

I took a deep breath before I admitted, "I think I was just mimicking my parent's relationship. Without realizing it, I was following in my mother's footsteps."

Mia looked at me, then added, "I believe that's what Oprah would call a lightbulb moment?"

I laughed. "Something like that, but I think you're right. I planned the damn party. Why shouldn't I enjoy it?"

Mia clapped her hands together. "All right! That's my girl! Now, we need to go shopping for some new outfits.

Operation: Make the Boys Sweat is underway," she said in a singsong voice as she floated to her bedroom.

I had a smile on my face even as uncertainty settled at the bottom of my stomach. If I was going to stop being the doormat I've become over the last few months, then I was going to have to make some big changes, no matter how uncomfortable they were. I already had a long list in my head of everything I needed to do to reclaim my life. But first, I needed to show up at that party and show Leo exactly what he was giving up.

"I don't think this is such a good idea anymore," I whined as we neared the lake house.

Mia looked over at me sharply. "I love you, but if you say that one more time, I'm going to have to give you a sisterly slap."

"You would really do that?"

"If it's what it takes to snap you out of this, then yes. It's all out of love, of course," she said.

I rolled my eyes and shook my head. "I'm getting more anxious the closer we get to the lake house. This will be the first time I have seen him since he dumped me, and I feel like such a loser."

"But you're not a loser and don't get in your head about this. Come on, you are dressed to the nines and you look sex-eee," she said, drawing out the last word. "I look pretty good too," she said.

I laughed. "We both look pretty good," I admitted.

"We are stunning, but what's going to make us go from looking good to knock out is how we walk into that party. So, tell me again," she insisted, wanting me to go over the plan for the hundredth time. It was getting annoying, but I couldn't blame her, considering how nervous I was.

I sucked in a long breath, then recited, "We go in head held high, hips swaying, and we talk to everyone but Leo."

"Exactly!" she said with a decisive head nod. "And, if you can find yourself a stud muffin and start chatting him up, that would be icing on the cake."

I laughed. "I don't know. I know most of Leo's friends. Some are cute, but I'm not sure any of them qualify as a stud muffin… where did that term come from, anyway? Your Grandmother?"

"Hey, Granny has some pearls of wisdom, so what if her terms are a little outdated?" she countered.

I relaxed and focused on Mia's words as we approached the lake house.

I'd been out here once before with Leo's parents, and it was beautiful. It was empty most of the time, and I knew his parents were thinking about turning it into a vacation rental for tourists. I'd had fun decorating the place for the party. There were several times in the last three weeks since I'd been in and out of the house setting up that I stopped to watch the sunset over the lake.

Although the house was a little big for my personal taste, it had a stunning view. When I looked out of the big plate-glass window in the living room towards the backyard, I spied a pier that stretched over the edge of the lake and led to a guesthouse. I hadn't seen the inside, but it looked like the perfect place to escape for a little while.

I knew that if I got overwhelmed during the party, I could look out the window and escape to the guesthouse on the water. I had even revealed this plan to Mia, who replied, "Don't you be escaping to that guesthouse. You need to stay present and hot—that is our mission."

When I looked a little terrified at the thought, she reminded me, "My phone is on me—the second you need to go, just text me and we will get the hell out of there."

I remembered that promise now and took comfort in it. I was so lucky to have her as my best friend. There is no way I'd survive this without her.

I rubbed my sweaty palms over my thighs, tugging at the short hem of my dress. It was a sexy little sundress that hit mid-thigh, with spaghetti straps over a peasant bodice with a little keyhole tie at the front, revealing an ample amount of cleavage. This is the most risqué dress I've ever owned, and it made me self-conscious. When I slipped it on in the store, Mia had assured me this was the dress that would make Leo eat his heart out. I paired it with some strappy sandals and swept my hair back into a French roll with loose curls framing my face. I felt overdressed for a causal lake house party—but we were going for sexy, and Mia assured me it was.

Every time I shifted in the car seat, I felt my boobs slip further out of my dress, and it was a little nerve-racking knowing I was revealing so much. When Leo and I had been together, I dressed more conservatively. This memory irritated me and made me stick out my chest a little more.

It was time to get the old Paige back and she never would have given a shit about how revealing this outfit was.

Mia found a place to park, and I took a deep breath before I stepped out of the car. She rushed around the front to grab my hand. "Remember who you are. You are Paige-fucking-Russell, a woman not to be messed with," she said in my ear as we walked into the party.

The place was already bustling, and the drinks were flowing. I noticed Leo had added a keg, which I had argued against when I planned the party, but I knew there would be a couple of bottles of wine in his parents' wine cabinet. I would find my way over there at some point. In the meantime, I girded my loins against the onslaught of rowdy partiers.

"Dammit, I should not have had that big ass soda before we got here," Mia said, squirming next to me.

"There's a bathroom down the hall to the left," I said, pointing toward the restroom.

She looked at me with uncertainty. "I do not want to leave you here alone."

I patted her on the shoulder. "I'm a big girl. Paige-fucking-Russell, remember? I'll be okay. Find me when you're done."

She gave me a grateful look and leaned in to say, "Nine o'clock. One of those stud muffins is checking you out. You can thank me later," she winked, rushing off to the bathroom.

My gaze went in the direction she had pointed and met a pair of intense, dark eyes that were watching me.

I felt the blush crawl down my body along with the man's eyes. He was tall, broad-shouldered, and shameless, by the way he was looking at me.

I swallowed around the nervous lump in my throat. I've never had a man look at me like that before. He looked unfamiliar to me—and older than everybody else here. I wondered who he was, as I turned to walk away.

I wandered through the house greeting people I recognized and congratulating the ones who were still sober enough to understand what I was saying.

As I slowly made my way to the wine cabinet off the side of the kitchen, I heard a playful giggling and a familiar voice.

I stopped in my tracks, following the sounds. It was coming from Leo's father's office. The door was ajar, and when I looked inside, I glimpsed an ass I recognized all too well—Leo's.

My eyes traveled upward, and I saw his ass drilling into a beautiful girl I recognized from one of his study groups. Her head was thrown back and her hands clutched his shoulders as he fucked her over the desk.

Everything inside of me went cold. Did they even realize the door was open, or did they just not care?

I sucked in a breath and got my feet to move, rushing away from the scene of the crime. Except it wasn't a crime, was it? Leo and I broke up. What he does now is none of my business.

I made it to the wine cabinet and selected my vintage of choice with a decisive flourish. I poured myself a generous glass, took a large sip and tried to erase the image replaying in my mind.

Leo had always wanted me to do something wild like that, but I didn't want to disrespect his parents' home, especially if I was going to be a part of the family.

We'd had plenty of sex, but we could never be too boisterous. There was always a roommate on the other side of the wall or his family down the hall.

He was always grooming me to be a lady—to conduct myself as someone who could be a future lawyer's wife. I had to be put together at all times. I guess now I understand what he meant when he called me a "cold fish." He wanted someone to bend over his father's desk. I didn't hate the idea, though now I hated the idea of it with him.

I looked up from behind the kitchen island and, once again, my mystery man's eyes were on me. He was much closer now, though still a respectable distance away. He was close enough now that I could tell they were dark brown... and they were looking at me like I was naked.

Emboldened by heartbreak and anger, I held his gaze as I brought my wineglass to my mouth again and took a healthy swallow. One side of his mouth quirked up, bringing my attention to his full lips. He had some stubble on his face, and suddenly I wondered what his stubble would feel like against my skin.

"Paige," a whisper came next to me, and I nearly jumped out of my skin. Mia was next to me now, and teased, "I see you and stud muffin have progressed to eye fucking. I have to say I'm proud of you."

Scan to get *Second Chance with My Ex's Brother* now!

Keep in Touch

W ant to stay up to date on all things Ana Rhodes? Join her newsletter! Get exclusive access to bonus content, cover reveals, excerpts, news and give-aways.

SCAN to subscribe!

Let's be friends on social media:
https://www.instagram.com/anarhodesauthor/
https://www.facebook.com/anarhodeswrites
https://www.goodreads.com/author/show/42608432.An
a_Rhodes

Printed in the USA
CPSIA information can be obtained
at www.ICGtesting.com
LVHW021433050624
782369LV00007B/24